Chasing New Suns

Collected Stories

Lance Robinson

Acknowledgements

The people who have helped me along in my writing journey over the years are too many to list, but I'll mention a few: Mark Leslie for his encouragement and guidance on the business of publishing; John, Joni, Meliva, Emily, Jody, Rob, and everyone who makes *Writers of the Future* happen; and Leland Sapiro who, years ago as the editor of *Riverside Quarterly*, published my first short story, "Communion", which is included in this volume. And everlasting thanks to my parents who, when I was fifteen years old, bought me a typewriter.

This book is for Elham and Richard.
You give me hope for a future brighter
than any I have imagined here.

Contents

Chasing New Suns

Five Days Until Sunset

1

Bering Stiles laid himself down in the hibetank, and as the sedative billowed into his thoughts, he whispered a prayer of thanksgiving and sank into nothingness. Then, with no clear sense of the passage of time, he felt his self rematerializing like a fog slowly solidifying.

Something's wrong.

Over a span of a few hours, drifting between stupor, sleep, confusion, and fleeting instances of clarity, he formed three slightly more complete thoughts. They came all at once—that he was not dead, that he was waking up, but disturbingly, that he was alone. There should have been doctors and their assistants at his side, monitoring his vitals, offering him water, and speaking soothing words. But there were no human beings darting in and out among the rows of hibetanks, only the inanimate arms, tubes and tentacles of med drones. It took another foggy while—he was not sure whether minutes or hours—before he realized something else.

No, not exactly alone.

At the fourth tank to his right another person was also awake, having just stood up from her tank. "We're on the planet," she croaked.

He considered answering her, but he was still fumbling to even string thoughts together, let alone words. As he pulled himself up to a sitting position, she did a deep knee bend, holding on to the side of her tank, then stood up straight again. Apparently, she had less of a hibernation hangover than he did. She cleared her throat. "Feel the gravity?"

She's . . . What's her name? I met her about a week before going into the tank. Naka . . . Right, Jeremy Nakamura. What did she say? The planet. The gravity. Bering lifted his arm and let it fall, realizing that she was right. The recon probe that had swung through the Epsindi system a century before he was born had estimated the surface gravity of Epsindi Ta to be thirteen percent higher than Earth's, and now he felt just a little heavier than he was used to.

This means we survived the voyage. We survived the 144 years in hibernation! We crossed light years!

None of these things had been certainties when they were put under. Bering silently repeated the same prayer of thanksgiving he had whispered one hundred forty-four years earlier—moments ago.

But questions began to taint his elation, and as she slipped on a robe, Frau Nakamura asked one of those questions as if reading his thoughts. "Why did the system wake *us*?"

He made no attempt to answer, not yet trusting his vocal cords. Then, as she began inspecting the other hibetanks, he took a few more deep breaths, swung his legs over the edge of his tank, and carefully stood up. Once he decided that he was not going to faint, he also put on a robe. Then he shuffled to a console, sat down, and began demanding answers.

"Where is . . . ?" He coughed up some phlegm then tried again. "Where is Dr. Kumarisov?"

<<That information is unavailable.>>

"Where are the members of the initial revival team?"

<<That information is unavailable.>>

"Where are we?"

<<Drop ferry *Assiniboine* touched down on Epsindi Ta three hours and forty-eight minutes ago at 65.3 degrees north latitude, 94.3 degrees east longitude.>>

Nakamura laughed. "I told you. We're not in the ark; we're on the planet."

"Frau Nakamura, this doesn't make sense. Something must have—"

A shrill claxon from one of the hibetanks startled them both, and immediately the ferry shot mnemonic scents into the air. Bering inhaled, letting the smell prime his memory, and then he realized why he, the youngest of the entire family of pilgrims, had been revived together with Jeremy Nakamura. His main contribution to the colony was to be engineering and construction, but like everyone, he had some training in other areas as well. His included astronomy, horticulture, and basic medicine, including hibernation revival.

As Nakamura moved to inspect the hibetank sounding an alarm, she again voiced what he was already thinking. "You and I—we're the alternates to the alternates. Kumarisov was meant to oversee the hibernation revivals. If the system needs us to revive the others, it means Dr. Kumarisov, Dr. Apshana, their assistants, everyone meant to serve on the initial revival team—they're . . ." Her voice trailed off, and Bering had no need to hear her finish the thought.

Before moving to help her, he checked the displays on three other hibetanks. At two of them, their fellow pilgrims were already in the preliminary stages of being revived. Bering's training, though narrow, was profound, having been cross-learned through qigonic meditation, olfactory priming, and hours of kinesthetic repetition, and it sprang up to guide him. By the time they had helped eight fellow pilgrims through stage four of the revival process, another eight were beginning stage four.

The ferry continued waking the pilgrims in batches. Bering and Nakamura did what they could to resolve the emergencies and calm those who awoke in confusion or panic. In each batch, at least one person asked, "Where's Dr. Kumarisov?" By the fourth time he heard the question, Bering was getting annoyed—not annoyed at the repetition so much as annoyed at being reminded of what the situation implied. *If the hibernation system called on the third alternates to do this, it means something went terribly wrong.*

But he had no time to dwell on that, because the revivals kept coming. Eventually, they learned that the other two drop ferries from the ark had also set down nearby. Someone from the *Serengeti* radioed, and it became clear that the same thing was also happening there and on the *Haida Gwaii*. Two people on each ferry revived first, then everyone else in stages.

As Bering attended to the successive waves of revivals, he heard someone from the first batch of patients try, as he had, to get information from a console. "Who ordered us revived?"

<<That information is unavailable.>>

"Where are the shuttles, *Guanahani* and *Beijing*?" They were smaller than *Assiniboine, Haida Gwaii* and *Serengeti,* and not equipped with hibetanks. If the initial revival team had been revived according to the default plan—ahead of everyone else while still in orbit on the ark—then they might have taken one of the smaller landers down to the planet surface.

<<That information is unavailable.>>

If the consoles don't know where the landers are, where the lead medical team is, or even who initiated this revival of everyone . . . Bering did not let himself think about what might have happened. He needed to concentrate. Someone in the last batch of revivals was hyperventilating.

As Bering helped her, one of the first people revived after him and Nakamura took readings of the external atmosphere and confirmed the recon probe's analysis, hundreds of years earlier—19.0% oxygen, 78.7% nitrogen, 1.5% argon, 0.4% neon, trace carbon dioxide, and nothing poisonous. It was slightly thicker than Earth's atmosphere, and so although as a percentage oxygen was less than on Earth, its partial pressure was actually higher—all-in-all, quite breathable.

Twenty-four hours after Bering regained consciousness, the successive waves of revivals had finished, and no one was left in hibernation. On the *Assiniboine*, two people could not be revived, and one revived, but then had a seizure and died. Between the three ferries, three hundred fifteen had been brought down to the planet surface, and by the time the last hibetank had been opened, two hundred eighty-eight emerged alive. But this meant not only that twenty-seven people died coming out of hibernation, but also that one hundred fifty-four were unaccounted for.

Once he had done everything he could for the last of the waking pilgrims, Bering stepped out of the ferry and found dozens of others all admiring a sublime sunset. Euphoria briefly lifted him above the questions and worries. The family of pilgrims had successfully escaped their oppression, left it one hundred thirteen trillion kilometers behind so that they could become humanity's first flowering beyond the Sol system. And Bering, having lived as an orphan and refugee, never being able to stay in one place for more than a few years, would finally build a home.

But what happened to the others? How can a hundred and fifty-four of us be missing? He pushed the doubts down. Then, his adrenaline spent, he laid down in the grass, ignoring the gentle breeze that caressed him to sleep.

2

Data, analysis, collective intuition, five different religious traditions, and the Promise of the Teacher who reunited those traditions have all told us that the time of human flowering has finally arrived. I am convinced now that this world can be one of the new gardens for our flowering. But instead of accepting the gift as it is, we fretted and dallied over Epsindi Ta's inconveniences for decades.

—From the journal of Adam Leifson

found at the fourth cairn

When, some hours later, someone woke Bering, birds were singing and the sun was still suspended on the western horizon. Seeing the sun sitting at the same point in the sky unsettled him even though rationally he understood it. Data sent back to the Sol system by the recon probe had suggested that the planet was tidally locked—an eyeball planet that permanently presented the same face toward its K5 orange dwarf star. The probe had swung by Epsindi

Ta only three times before going silent, and the data it returned were scanty. Nevertheless, thermographic analysis assessed the temperature at the substellar point—the longitude experiencing permanent noon—to be seventy-nine degrees Celsius, while the night side of the planet was nearly cold enough for carbon dioxide to freeze out.

But the data had also shown that in the planet's twilight ring, where the day-night cycle was suspended in a never-ending sunrise/sunset, photosynthetic life thrived. Bering's faith in the Promise of humanity's flowering was strong, but this world would be a strange fulfillment of that Promise. A place where time felt different, where day and night were undesirable destinations rather than markers on the flow of time. Nevertheless, signs of the Promise were all around him. He was breathing the air, the temperature was perfect, and the bed of grass and flowers that he had slept on was evidently Earth flora. And he was hearing birds! And, not only was he hearing birds, but the trill call and a check-check-check response was completely familiar.

Those are red-winged blackbirds! But how?

For his whole life, Bering had fled from place to place, hidden from mobs and from men in uniform, and been shunted first from one orphanage to another and then from one refugee camp to another. His faith in the Teacher and in the Promise had kept him going, but never had he imagined that the Promise would be so bounteously fulfilled.

But he had no time to marvel at how this planet was teeming with what seemed to be Earth life, or to appreciate the permanently paused beauty of the sunset, or to meditate on the play of light and shadow across what seemed to be trees on the hills to the south. A concourse had been called, and the two hundred eighty-eight pilgrims were gathering on the grassy plain between the *Haida Gwaii* and the *Serengeti*.

First, the names of the twenty-seven who had died were announced, and a hymn chanted. This was more than they had hoped to lose to the risky hibernation process, but still within the range they expected, so the voyage could only be considered a success, and prayers of praise, thanksgiving, and anticipation were offered from three of the five religious traditions represented among their number. Then Fatuma Chisholm, one of the deputies elected to the family council before the voyage and the person presiding over the concourse, explained what Bering already knew. The consoles on the ferries either lacked or had been instructed not to provide what should have been straightforward information.

"Nevertheless," she called in a loud voice so everyone could hear, "we have made two important discoveries." She pointed to her right. "First, look over there. There at the midpoint between the three ferries. It's barely visible from here, but there's a small mound. It's a pile of rocks in fact, and though it isn't obvious from here, it's actually a cairn. The rocks were stacked up that way by human hands. Our ferries landed in a triangle because each landed 290 meters from the cairn and a safe distance from each other. The rocks were protecting a radio beacon—a beacon set there by a fellow pilgrim to direct us here."

"So, the missing brothers and sisters," someone called out, "they're not dead?"

"Well, that brings us to the second discovery. We examined the beacon. It was placed there a long time ago and set with a timer. And from the control systems of the hibetanks, we confirmed the information from the beacon." She took a deep breath. "Our hibernation did not last one hundred forty-four years. It's been three hundred and eighty-four. We arrived in orbit around Epsindi Ta two hundred and forty years ago."

There were scattered gasps, and then silence settled over the assembled concourse. This meant it was not only the twenty-seven who were dead, but also the missing hundred and fifty-four. Even if every single one of them survived revival, they had all died of old age more than a century ago.

As they absorbed the news, some people cried and some comforted each other in twos and threes. Bering stared off at nothing, thinking of Ulysses Degana, his mentor, and one of only two people in the whole ark family he had known before being selected for the crew. It was Degana who had vouched for him in the crew selection process. But Bering knew that for some, the loss was much worse—some of the pilgrims had spouses among the hundred and fifty-four.

After a suitable pause, Frau Chisholm called for silence. She initiated a discussion of practicalities, but agreement was elusive. Did their fellow pilgrims who preceded them intend for them to build the village here, or was this a location chosen randomly by a malfunctioning semi-mind on the ark? Several people voiced their impatience to activate the default settlement plan and start building. Eventually, however, they reached consensus that first they needed to learn more. Once that was decided, most of the two hundred eighty-eight easily fell into one of two broad groups. One group had the task of investigating, of finding out whatever they could about what had gone wrong. As the concourse concluded, leaders of various investigation teams—geology, climatology, biology, edaphology, ships' engineering, and others—shouted out to assemble their teams.

Bering knew he belonged in the second group: those who would support the first group, preparing food and temporary shelter, providing medical and spiritual care, and managing logistics. His primary role in the family was to be engineering and construction, and even for a temporary camp there would be printing and fabricating to be done and shelters to be built. For the next few hours, Bering worked with one of the engineering teams setting up a hydroponics system. At first, they were entirely focused on the work in front of them, but as they fell into a rhythm, conversation soon zeroed in on the oddities in their revival, the uncooperative consoles, and the missing hundred fifty-four members of their family.

Ford Cyltemstra, the deputy head of engineering, made it clear that he thought there was no point worrying about it. "Beaumont or Elysium will reestablish contact with the ark. They'll figure it out when they figure it out." He spoke to Bering and the others of his hopes and plans for their life in this new world and his confidence in all the preparation the family and their fellow believers back on Earth had done. He framed these thoughts mostly using the terminology of his Francisco-Nasrian Faith—the same as Bering's—but also pausing to draw connections to beliefs and concepts from the other four religious traditions of the family. His faith in the Promise shone, but it could not lift Bering away from his disquiet over the unanswered questions. So, when the team finished the hydroponics installation and Ford announced a short break, Bering took his assistant from his pocket and asked it to locate Taamir Beaumont.

He found the elder alone in a flat grassy field two hundred meters from the *Assiniboine*, assembling an antenna. Beaumont's weathered face and greying hair only hinted at his age. Although most of the pilgrims selected for the ark were between twenty-five and forty-five years old, Bering knew that forty years before their journey even began, Beaumont had spent decades designing the engine that powered the ark.

"Sen. Beaumont."

The old man looked up. "Sen. Stiles."

"Yes, sir. Sen. Beaumont sir, I have training in astronomy."

"I know; I was on the committee that selected you for the ark when an opening came up. But, don't you have construction work to do?"

"I do. But something went wrong here—something with our arrival in this system, or with the landing, or something—and the sooner we find out what it was, the better."

Beaumont looked down at the antennas at his feet, then looked back up. "Absolutely. And as it turns out, everyone else with training in astronomy was among the hundred fifty-four, so you and I, the oldest and the youngest of the entire family—we're all that remains of the astronomy team. So, I guess I better say yes. Not that our new culture on this world will do much astronomy, at least not visual astronomy."

"We could eventually build observatories on the night side of the planet," Bering offered. "Not at the midnight point, but somewhere where the cold is at least manageable."

"One day, Sen. Stiles. But for now, the only star we can observe in the visible spectrum is that one." He pointed to the orange orb that still hung on the western horizon, now partly obscured by a thin stratus cloud. "We can use some prehistoric astrometric techniques. Do you know how to measure the angular size of our new sun in the sky?"

Bering nodded vigorously.

"Good. We should confirm if the recon probe data about the size of the star and our distance from it are correct. But you can do that later. First, help me set up this radio array. You can use it to start making images of the sky."

It took the two of them a little over two hours to set up the array of half-meter antennas, Bering doing most of the physical labor as Sen. Beaumont stopped frequently to rest. They instructed the antennas to upload their data to a console in the *Assiniboine*, then entered the ferry and confirmed that the data was arriving and being saved.

When they stepped back outside, Bering noticed that the breeze had died down, and looking to the west he saw that clouds had formed, blocking the view of their new sun.

"Interesting," Beaumont remarked.

"I thought the weather was going to be absolutely constant here. No planetary rotation, no day and night, no moons, and no axial tilt—so no changes in weather."

"It seems we have much to learn. But as for measuring the width of Epsindi, that will have to wait until the sky clears."

"Sen. Beaumont, why do you think we were set down somewhere different than the first pilgrims? And why would a fellow pilgrim have set the timer on that beacon for two hundred forty years?"

"In the concourse, Fatuma was preoccupied with sharing the bad news and with how people would react, so she omitted some of the finer details. Actually, the timer wasn't set until about forty-five years after the ark arrived in orbit. And then it was set for 194.89 years, as were timers in each of the three drop ferries. So, for some reason, our brothers and sisters were here for forty-five years and saw fit not to revive us. And, then in planting the beacon and giving instructions to the ferries, they decided we needed to wait another one hundred ninety-five years. As for 'why?'—that question has my mind spinning. It's what we're all trying to find out. Maybe this…"—he gestured toward the antenna array—"maybe this will give us some clues. In the meantime, I think you should get back to your construction team."

Contamination! I forgot to message Ford.

Bering went running back to the hydroponics installation and the main site of their new camp, but the others had ended work for the day. He checked his pocket assistant. There were no messages, but there were several broadcast announcements. One of them explained that with no planetary day and night cycle to shepherd their circadian rhythms, a standard time had been set and was now synchronized to everyone's assistant. He checked and saw that the time now was six and a half hours after standard noon. That gave him an idea of where he might find Ford. He went straight to the tent designated as a dining hall and found him there just finishing his meal. As Bering took a chair beside him, Ford looked at him but said nothing. Bering quickly explained and tried to apologize, but Ford stood up, interrupting.

"Being a pilgrim is a responsibility and a gift," he said, then left the tent.

Bering ate in silence: crackers with lentil paste and a bland, grey vatcake.

By the time he was done, a fog was descending over their camp and the temperature had dropped at least a degree—another subtle deviation from what he had been led to expect here. It joined the other anomalies and questions swirling around in his mind as he went to find a sleeping mat in one of the tents.

3

Because of the disasters that beset us, most caused by our own inaction, I was left with little choice but to then add another nineteen and a half decades to your sleep. One hundred ninety-five years—or should I say "thirteen days"?—was my best estimate of where to strike the balance between the danger of extending your time in hibernation versus giving the semi-mind on the ark, and the gene lab and incubators it is guiding, enough time to do their work.

Before you curse me for imposing that calculation upon you, know that where you set down is an Eden compared to where we first tried to start the colony. That most of this planet is, in its own way, a paradise is almost certainly thanks to a seed ship. Sent out thirteen thousand years ago before the Dark Ages at the end of the anthropo-unification era when, for a brief eight or ten centuries, humanity was united, the legend says the seed ships were the only attempt the ancients made at interstellar travel before the Chaos. They carried flora and fauna, a great DNA library and artificial wombs of various sorts, but no human passengers. One of those ships certainly must have come here to Epsindi Ta. The seed that it planted was the Promise.

For thirteen millennia, the seed ship prepared this world for us, and like a child copying its mother, I have added another thirteen days, enough time, I pray, to make a few small additions to this garden.

—From the second cairn epistle of
Adam Leifson to the third generation

Waking early, Bering quietly dressed so as not to disturb those who were still sleeping, and stepped out of his dorm tent. Clearly, members of one of the other building teams had not slept at all. More large tents and some prefab panel structures had been erected. Then when he reached the dining tent, he saw that someone had hung two rows of luzglobes—with the sun still obscured by haze and clouds, the natural light was not enough. Permanent structures were yet to come, but already the camp was starting to look like their new home.

Among the other early risers in the dining tent, he saw Jaykella Tahirani. Aside from Ulysses Degana, she was the only other fellow pilgrim he had known before being selected for the ark, essentially at the last minute—only four weeks before departure. They had been together as youths in the same refugee camp after fleeing the pogroms. Bering sat down. She introduced him to the two people she was sitting with, both of them part of the same biology team as her. Gopal Nairobiani was a handsome, athletic-looking guy—in his mid-thirties, Bering guessed—but Arsen Kazakii was younger; he could hardly be older than Bering himself.

"Has your team learned anything about the ecology here?" Bering asked.

"We've only been here one day," Jaykella answered with a laugh. "But, yeah, we've learned a few things. Except for some moss, everything's completely familiar—plants *and* animals. It's not just that they're related to Earth life; they're all known species."

"Are ya knowin', man, about the legend of the seed ships?" Arsen asked in a thick belt colony accent.

"The life we're seeing was brought here by a seed ship?"

"I bin sequencin' the genomes," Arsen said. "That might be tellin' us. In fact, I need to go see if my first analyses are finished. The team leader has a meetin' with the other team leaders at the cairn in a few minutes."

"Wait. First tell me what else you found. Did you find any clues about what happened to the rest of the family?"

Jaykella answered. "Nothing about what happened to them, but we have learned some interesting stuff. For instance, almost all the animals I saw on my transects are migratory species. Some of the insect species aren't but, every bird species I saw is migratory. So that's kinda strange."

"Why do you say that?"

"The planet doesn't have a day and night cycle, and it doesn't have seasons, as far as we know. But all the birds I saw were flying west. Even the antelopes I saw were moving west too."

"I think I saw wild goats," said Gopal. "But they were far away."

"It was probably the same antelopes," Jaykella replied. "But, the question is, if there's no weather and no seasons, why migrate? But team leader Watersmith wasn't interested. He just wanted to know what plants could be weeds to the crops we'll grow and what animals will be pests."

Gopal leaned forward. "So many of the plants we found—wow!—so, so many are edible."

"Right," Arsen said. "That means if the farmin' is hard, we can add bits'a variety by foragin'. But, man, the real question is, if the life we're seein' was placed here by a seed ship from Earth, aren't these all invasive species?" At first, Bering thought he had heard Arsen wrong, but he went on. "And if they're invasive species, doesn't that make us the second wave of the invasion?"

"Invasive species?" Bering blurted. "No. The real question is 'How are we going to live on this world?'" He jumped to his feet. "Invasive species? This world is the gift promised for us!"

He shocked himself with the intensity of his reaction, and clearly, he jarred Jaykella, Arsen, and Gopal as well. Embarrassed, he used their surprise as an opportunity to stride away. But the more he thought about what Arsen had said, the more he felt justified. *How can he suggest we don't belong here? He can question the Promise if he wants, but I won't. We're building our new home here, and nothing is going to stop that.*

And so, as Bering reached the *Assiniboine*, he resolved to keep learning what he could, and follow through with the astronomical observations. If he was quick, he could still join his construction team before they even got breakfast. He wanted to do the measurement of Epsindi's apparent diameter, but although the fog had lifted in the vicinity of the ships, to the west the sky was still hazy, so he would have to wait a little longer.

But not much longer, he told himself as he noticed sunlight illuminating the peaks of the hills to the south.

Just then a chill ran through him.

"Yeah, it cooled off a little," a woman remarked, stepping out of the ferry. "I thought the weather here wasn't supposed to change."

Bering glanced over to her and shrugged, then snapped his attention back to the hills. It *was* slightly cooler, but that was not what had given him the chill. Something in what he was seeing was not right. In the light and shadow on the hills, there was something out of place. He looked to the west, then looked back to the hills one more time, and promised himself he would come back to meditate in view of those hills later. For now, he went into the *Assiniboine* to check on the radio telescope data. It had only been thirteen hours since he and Sen. Beaumont had finished setting it up, so only the first small square of the sky would have been imaged. Now in its second twelve-hour scan, the array would be observing the next square. It would take nine weeks this way to do a complete picture of the sky, but Bering wanted to confirm that everything was working. Rushing to a console, he almost knocked over a glass with some wildflowers that someone had picked. He steadied it, moved it aside, then called up the radio array data. He instructed the console to present the data for the first section of observed sky as a single image, the range of radio frequencies to be displayed as visible colors using the default conversion. Remembering his first hours out of the hibetank, he half expected to be told "that information is unavailable," or perhaps to see a meaningless jumble or a black screen as a result of some technical fault or some mistake he might have made, but to his relief, a recognizable image appeared. Cutting across one corner of the image was the plane of the galaxy, a bright line interspersed with brighter spots along it. Ionized interstellar gas appeared as glowing wisps, and other bright dots—supernova remnants and distant radio galaxies—were scattered here and there.

However, the image was not as sharp as it should have been, and looking at a few of the dots, he saw the problem. They were not dots but short lines, all the same length, all oriented in the same direction, as if the objects had tracked faster across the sky than the radio array had accounted for. Even if the planet was locked to its star, it was still rotating as it orbited the star, rotating once for each of its years, and that meant that in the twelve hours it took to scan one patch of sky, relative to the stars the planet had turned just a little. This should have already been compensated for, but apparently some mistake had been made, otherwise the stars would have been crisp dots rather than short lines.

He confirmed what planetary rotation rate had been used in assembling the data: 317.96 Earth days, the same as the planet's orbital period. That should have been correct. Then he instructed the console to work at the problem backward—to create a second image, aligning the data from across the twelve-hour period and then determine what rotation rate that corresponded to. The answer came—300.54 Earth days. The difference was small—small, but detectable, a little over three one hundredths of a degree difference, but that was enough to make the stars and other radio-bright objects appear as short lines rather than points.

Bering's past forty-eight hours suddenly collapsed together into a singular understanding—the light and shadow on the hills, the shifting weather, the miscalculated radio array image, and even Jaykella's fascination with migratory species. He stared at the number on the display—300.54 Earth days. Any lingering grogginess disappeared and all his senses snapped, like the second radio telescope image, into crisp focus. He felt the soft cushion of the chair under him, smelt a faint aroma from the flowers, and heard the fans of the ferry's air circulation system.

And his beating heart.

He transferred the data and the two images—the original blurred image and the corrected one—to a portable screen, then jumped from the chair and sprinted out of the ferry.

He ran toward the center point of the triangle between the three ferries. The wind was picking up again, and it carried away the small dust clouds he kicked up from the dry prairie as he ran.

Ten council members were sitting in a circle on the ground near the cairn that the three ferries had centered themselves around. A few meters away on the far side of the cairn, an eleventh, Frau Annamiek Ismail, appeared to be looking for something in the grass. When Bering got close, he stopped a respectful distance away and waited. They all glanced his way, then continued their deliberations. He waited, catching his breath while making sure that the portable screen he had brought from the ferry was ready.

"As I was saying," Youssou Watersmith explained to the council, "we have sequenced twenty-two flora genomes and two insect genomes. Among those, there was one lichen and one fungus which, based on genetic drift, are separated from any known species in our library by millions of years at least—they're probably native to this world. But for all the rest, the genetic drift suggests they diverged from known Earth species only 13,200 years ago, plus or minus 350 years. Several of them have anomalies that I suspect, way back then, were engineered, but across the bulk of the noncoding and mitochondrial DNA, they have consistently drifted 13,200 years. So, I would say that some version of the seed ship legend is true."

Fatuma Chisholm stood up. "Thank you, Sen. Watersmith. Is that all?" Watersmith nodded and Frau Chisholm called to Bering. "Young Sen. Stiles, are you delivering a message, or do you want to join our deliberations? What is it?"

"Well, um, I found something."

"Don't just stand there; come closer."

Frau Chisholm sat down, but when Bering reached the circle, he remained standing.

Then, after a few seconds of silence, all of them staring at him, he realized he did not need any further permission to speak and that they were waiting for him.

"So, umm, I was checking the radio telescope array, and I found something—something important. First, it was the wildlife Jaykella told me about. Every single bird species she saw is a migratory species, and also an antelope species, and they were all moving west."

"Bering," Youssou Watersmith bellowed, "are you talking about your radio telescope or the wildlife? Please. We're busy with important things here."

Taamir Beaumont spoke up. "Let him finish." Then he turned to Bering. "But please get to the point."

Don't babble, he told himself. *They need to understand this is important.*

"Sorry," he said. "I also noticed it's getting colder, and there seems to be too much weather. And that's when I checked the first image from our radio array. The image didn't track correctly." Bering realized that Sen. Beaumont would understand, but that he would have to explain more carefully for some of the others. "It's like this. The receivers don't take an instantaneous snapshot. They're meant to track the stars as the planet slowly turns. And in that time, they collect photons for twelve hours. But the image was streaked. It didn't track properly." He stepped over to Beaumont and gave him the portable screen.

Beaumont examined the image. "I must have made an error in setting it up."

"Yes and no, Sen. The error is easily corrected if we give the planet a sidereal day of 300.5 Earth days instead of 318." Beaumont's eyes went wide. Bering pointed to the south. "And those hills—that tallest hill there, it has a shadow cast on it from that smaller hill on the right. That shadow has been slowly moving."

Fatuma Chisholm pressed her hands together in front of her mouth.

"I don't understand," said Jeremy Nakamura, looking quickly from Chisholm, to Bering, to Beaumont, and back to Bering again. "What does all that mean?"

"It means the planet is rotating. Very slowly—"

"Yes," Watersmith interjected. "It rotates exactly once for each of its orbits around Epsindi."

"No, Sen.," explained Bering. "It's rotating just a little bit faster than that."

One of the other councillors sitting on Bering's left began whispering, "No, no, no, no."

"Bering, are you saying this isn't an eyeball planet?" Jeremy Nakamura demanded.

Taamir Beaumont answered for him. "At this incredibly slow rate of rotation, it's definitely an eyeball planet. The probe sent back infrared images and measured the temperature at the substellar point to be seventy-nine degrees Celsius. And on the night side, we know it was colder than minus fifty."

"The recon probe went silent after a short time in this system," Bering added. "If it had functioned longer, we would have had more data, and maybe people would have realized. But this means the planet is not tidally locked."

"It means," Beaumont said, "this planet has a day and a night. A day lasts . . ." He looked down to the portable screen and tapped a calculation into it, then looked up. "About fifteen Earth years."

"Taamir," Youssou Watersmith pleaded, "this can't be right."

Frau Ismail—the council member who was not sitting in the circle but was standing on the far side of the cairn—spoke up. "It *is* right. Come here, everyone, and I'll show you." They hesitated, and she said it again, "Come. Here." The councillors all rose, and together with Bering walked over to Frau Ismail and gathered around her. "There are rocks laid out in lines in the grass. It's so overgrown it's hard to see them at all, but they are definitely arranged."

She pointed down to a line of rocks at her feet. "This isn't natural; I imagine they were placed this way by our same pilgrim sister or brother who put the beacon into this cairn two centuries ago."

She traced the lines the rocks made—two parallel lines of rocks a little over a meter long joined by a third, diagonal line. "Alef," she announced, and then pointed to another arrangement of rocks to the left. "Miim." And then another and another. "Double-jay. Omega. Omega. These are letters." She pointed out all the symbols, laid out in two rows each about six meters long.

"What does it all say?" someone asked.

Then Bering and several others saw that Rosa Okonkwo was now pointing, her lips quivering but not making a sound. They all turned in the direction she pointed, to the west. The haze on the horizon had begun to clear and the setting K5 sun was visible again. In that moment, Bering realized that part of him had been hoping that he was wrong, that Sen. Beaumont would explain some simple thing he had misconstrued, but now that faint hope was smashed. They all stood gazing at the star. When they had first emerged from the ferries, just the tip of it had settled below the horizon, but now, almost half of it had sunk out of view.

"What does the message say?" Frau Ismail echoed. "It says, 'Go west. Start walking.'"

4

We have taken to referring to ourselves as "generations" even though our actual ages had nothing to do with who got revived when. The first generation, observing our new home from orbit and realizing our conclusions about it being tidally locked were wrong, decided to locate the settlement at the North Pole. It was the only place we could build to avoid the day-night cycle and its 130-degree temperature swing. I was in the second "generation," and awoke to see my friends had aged twenty years and had run out of hope.

Sadly, my generation made just as many mistakes. And we were just as stubborn as the first, clinging to our expectations for our lives on this world. I pray that you in the third generation, separated from the site of our mistakes by 3000 kilometers and 195 years, will be able to do things better than we did.

—From the third cairn epistle of
Adam Leifson to the third generation

By the time the council called the whole family together for another concourse, the news had already spread. And, of course, with the sky clear, everyone could once again see the sun, see that it was slowly setting. Calculations also hinted at the significance of why the timers in the ferries and in the beacon had been set for 194.89 Earth years. It was equivalent to almost exactly thirteen planetary days.

But why not one day? Bering wondered. *Or two? Thirteen days is a hundred and ninety-five years. Why leave us that long?*

The questions were accumulating faster than answers could be found, and the gathering lurched and stumbled from one question to another and back again. If they believed what their eyes and calculations told them, that a day on this planet lasted fifteen years, and if they accepted the message written in the arrangement of rocks—"Go west; start walking"—what would that mean?

"We would walk and set up a new camp every few days," came the answer. "No village to eventually grow into a city. No new civilization. No permanent home."

"It means we would become primitives. Hunter-gatherer nomads."

"Maybe there was a mistake, a miscalculation."

"How can we travel twelve light years and not establish our colony?"

And so, they agonized over how they might build in order to survive the seven-year-long days and the seven-

year-long nights. They considered domes and underground habitats. They considered trying to construct
climate-protected greenhouses, and they considered
eating vat-grown food for the rest of their lives since
farming might be impossible. People who had a poor
sense of the limitations of their abilities, even asked about
finding a way to slow the planet's rotation to finish the
process of tidal locking. In the concourse, and in small
conversations afterward, they also talked about trying to
retrofit the drop ferries. The three large ferries were
designed as descent vehicles, meant to drop to the planet
surface once, but perhaps a way could be found to enable
at least one of them to fly again and they could use it to
relocate to the North Pole. The rough map created from
the recon probe's data had shown the South Pole to be a
sea, so the North Pole seemed the obvious choice. In fact,
it was such an obvious choice that it led people to ask,
"Why didn't the ark set us down there?"

The answer came a day later when a data grain was
found, wrapped in a piece of cloth and sealed inside a jar
that was sealed inside another jar and interred deeper
down in the cairn below where the beacon had been. It
held gigas of data and hundreds of pages of notes on
climate, ecology, physical geography, and geology, but the
team tasked with sifting through it had found no executive

summary, no editorial, no direct explanation or instructions. So the council copied it and distributed it to multiple teams, each assigned to comb through a different part of it, and when they did, a picture of the polar regions emerged. The data grain belonged to Adam Leifson, a member of the family's agriculture team who had been thirty-two years old when he went into hibernation.

According to his notes in the data grain, the first wave of pilgrims—the first "generation"—had learned that Earth life thrived everywhere on the planet except at the poles. Within one thousand kilometers of the poles was the only place where the original endemic ecosystems still survived, little affected by the species brought from Earth by the seed ship thirteen thousand years earlier. Although the poles did not experience the fifteen-year-long cycle of temperature extremes that the rest of the planet did, the weather there was chaotic and abrupt, often lurching from forty degrees above freezing to thirty degrees below within a few days, and then back again. Leifson's notes described tornados, which were common near the pole. And, in another section of the notes, Taamir Beaumont found a passing reference to coronal mass ejections from the star, geomagnetic storms focused on the poles, and damage to the earlier pilgrims' electrical systems.

"This is why we don't see any sign of the hundred fifty-four," Fatuma Chisholm speculated during the third concourse. "Or the smaller ferries or the cargo landers. They're at the North Pole. They tried to establish the colony there. They couldn't."

"It's unlivable," Frau Ismail added. "So, they never revived us. But Adam eventually told the ark to wait thirteen more of this planet's days and then put us here."

To Bering, this felt like a betrayal. He had devoted himself to the cause and to the Promise that the human race was ready to begin building a new home. He had dedicated himself to the precepts of that Promise: that it was not a largess bestowed from above, but a mission the pilgrims, and their fellow believers back on Earth, would carry out with perseverance and sacrifice; that they would live in harmony with the new worlds they reached; and that they would do better than what had been done on Earth. And, not having dared to hope that he himself would be chosen as a pilgrim, he had been rewarded, only four weeks before departure, by being added to the body of pilgrims bound for Epsindi Ta. He would finally have a permanent home, and as a junior engineer, his role in the family would be to literally help build that home.

But now, it felt as if someone was trying to take that from him. There was not even any work for him to do so that he could at least feel useful. The temporary shelters had already been built, and half the pilgrims chose to sleep on the ferries anyway. From bits and pieces of conversation he overheard over the next twenty-four hours, he learned that many people were feeling similarly betrayed. Some seemed sad, some frustrated, some angry. Many were defiant, insisting they could still find a way to move ahead with their plans to build a colony, a few even suggesting that some mistake had been made and that the apparent rotation of the planet was just a wobble or some other astronomical anomaly that had momentarily deceived them. It was those sentiments that felt most like his own as he fantasized about standing in front of someone and saying, "No! You won't take this from me!"

Some people were calling the situation a crisis, but for Bering it was simply incomprehensible. He could not make sense of it, so instead he focused his thoughts on imagining the colony post-crisis. Someone would come up with a clever mix of technologies to solve the puzzle, and then the current confusion would be just a memory.

5

Our generation waited too long. We delayed until we had no choice but to leave you with no choice. Please forgive us.

—From the second cairn epistle of
Adam Leifson to the third generation

When only a quarter of Epsindi remained visible above the horizon, another concourse was held, at which options already rejected were revisited and rejected again. Factions began to cleave the family. Those who felt they needed to immediately start moving the camp westward were the most emotional but were in the minority. For most, the response to that was simple and straightforward, "What you're suggesting is impossible."

"Three and a half years from now, the temperature here is going to be fifty degrees below freezing! And eleven years from now, it's going to be seventy-five degrees above freezing. Blindly following our plan is what's impossible! Adapting the plan and learning to live a different way—that's just inconvenient."

"So, you're saying we came to this planet to live like primitive nomads? No. I don't believe it."

Watching the fourth concourse go on like that, the deliberation becoming debate, the debate becoming mere contradiction, hit Bering viscerally. This was not the way the family was meant to operate. No one seemed to care that with each new opinion and pronouncement they were sowing strife, contention, and estrangement. Bering noticed, though, that these new cleavages did not follow the divisions between the family's five religious traditions in any way. He could not decide if that was a good sign or simply an ironic accident. *Briefly reunited just so we could find a new way to rip ourselves apart again.*

From what he could discern, the concourse ended with no real strategy. And during all this time, for two full days—two days by Earth reckoning he reminded himself, because an actual day on this world was five thousand times longer—he hardly spoke to anyone. He thought about the home he had imagined helping to build, about the Promise that had seemed for a moment to be abundantly fulfilled, and about what the Promise really meant if it was only going to be fleetingly fulfilled once every seven and a half years.

Eventually, however, he needed to share his feelings, to hear someone tell him, "Yes! Exactly!" And so, when he saw Jaykella Tahirani, the closest thing he had to a friend among the pilgrims still alive, sitting with a group of five others, he went toward them, hoping to find someone who might share, or at least empathize with, his confusion. Sitting beside Jaykella was one of the council members, Frau Annamiek Ismail, and there were three young pilgrims whose names he had not yet learned. And there was Arsen Kazakii. Remembering Arsen's disrespect of the Promise, Bering decided to just move along. But then, Jaykella saw him and invited him to sit.

"I want you to see something."

As he joined their circle, he saw that several items were spread out on the ground in front of them. The word *artifacts* came to mind. There were also neatly organized piles of various berries, mushrooms, and leaves.

"Bering's from Assiniboine," Jaykella told the others.

"I know," a tall redheaded woman replied. "He helped me get through a panic attack when I revived."

Bering did not remember her. Those first hours were all a blur.

"I don't mean he's from *the Assiniboine*," Jaykella said. "No, he's actually *from* Assiniboine, in the North American plains."

"From age six to age fifteen," Bering hedged. "I had to flee when the pogroms started. But yeah, I guess I'm from there as much as I'm from anywhere."

"Good!" Frau Ismail proclaimed, snapping her fingers as if in celebration. "A lot of the flora in this valley is native to your region. From our drones, it seems that twenty kilometers south, it's mostly African species, and twenty kilometers north, there's a mix from various places. But here, mostly species from the North American prairie."

She pointed to a small pile of purple berries. "Do you recognize these? They're not blueberries."

Bering looked, then picked up a few and popped them in his mouth.

"Hey! We haven't tested those!" Jaykella blurted.

"They might be poisonous," Frau Ismail added.

Bering looked at each of them in turn as he squished the berries around inside his mouth. The gentle sweetness seemed to spread from his tongue to his whole body and then blended with a nutty, earthy flavor. The taste took him back fifteen years to his childhood—summer in the valley, canoeing on the lake, Frau Harris's berry crumble. "They're Saskatoon berries."

"Saskatoon berries?" someone asked.

"They're named after the philosopher from the early Dark Ages, Jonathan Saskatoon."

"What about these mushrooms?" Jaykella asked. "Are they edible?"

"Oh, for wild mushrooms, I wouldn't know. But aren't most of you ecologists or biologists or whatever? All I know is what I learned in summer programs at the orphanage."

Jaykella had no chance to respond. "Bering," Frau Ismail said, motioning toward some very old looking pouches, sticks and jars, "we found these in a cave. In the hills south of here. We think they belonged to Adam Leifson. The jars and bags had some dried food—almost two hundred years old." Then she pointed to the fresh berries, mushrooms, and leaves. "For each one we could identify, we tried to collect fresh specimens of the same thing."

"From our surveys, we found twenty-nine edible species so far," said Arsen. "Thirty if we can be confirmin' the mushrooms."

"There were goose bones and antelope bones in the cave too," the redhead added. She picked up a stick about three centimeters in diameter and almost a meter long with a hook and notch at one end and a groove running almost the full length on one side. "This is an atlatl—a spear thrower."

Jaykella pointed to two thinner and much longer, very straight sticks. "It's used together with these."

Bering picked one up. A shaped point was attached to one end.

"They're darts for the atlatl," the redhead explained. "The points are ground from pieces of carbon-resin composite. Maybe from a seat or a cabinet from one of the missing shuttles. And there was a handheld pheromoner—he may have been using that to help with his hunting."

The group broke into an excited discussion about learning to tan hides, their willingness or unwillingness to learn how to eat meat, and whether the owner of the items had in fact walked all the way around the planet following the setting sun.

"Man, we can actually do this," Arsen said.

"It looks as if Adam was alone," Frau Ismail added. "But we'll be working together—strength in numbers—so, yes, we can do it."

"If we stay put," Jaykella added, "we'll freeze to death in the dark. We change our plans. That's all there is to it."

Bering decided this was not the kind of conversation he had been looking for. *They actually sound as if they're glad to tell the rest of us we can't stay and start growing our crops, can't start building our home.* So he made an excuse and then slipped away. He walked away from the group, away from the three ferries and from their camp, once again wanting to be alone. He headed northward. *Any direction but west.*

He had joined the family to have a chance at something he had been denied until now—a home. But they had come to a world that was telling him he had to become a nomad, perpetually homeless, perpetually chasing the sun. No, he would not go west.

And so, he walked north. He walked nearly three kilometers until he reached the edge of the wide valley where they had landed, and then began to hike up into the hills. Once he felt he had come far enough, he chose one hill and began to hike toward the top. As he ascended, the bushes became thicker, and eventually were an impenetrable thicket.

Choosing a grassy spot below the thick tangle of bushes, he turned to face west, and sat. For a moment he peered at the sliver of the star that was still visible above the horizon, but knowing that, like the Promise itself, it was slowly leaving them behind, he could not bear to keep looking. So as he began to pray, he closed his eyes.

He chose one of the prayers of flowering, "Your grace is plenteous; it cannot be veiled. We have abased ourselves, but with Your help we now arise. With wings that You bestowed, we soar now to our new habitation. We are Your seed, make us now worthy to flower. Make us worthy to recognize Your gift. We will accept that gift and become part of it."

The prayer seemed to bring some clarity, but no peace. He knew what they had to do. They all did. According to the legends, thirteen thousand years earlier, shortly before the end of the millennium-long era during which the human race had been united, humanity had engaged in a series of grand collective projects, beginning with restoration of the Earth and ending with the dispatching of ten or perhaps twelve automated ships that would seed other worlds. The pilgrims were agreed on at least one thing—that one of those ships had arrived here and begun preparing this world for them, making subtle adjustments to the genomes of the Earth life it chose from its libraries to ensure that each of the plants and animals it placed here would migrate, or be blown on the wind, or would set long lasting spores and seeds that would wait through the long cold nights and the long hot days. And the biology team kept finding edible species. The climate was gentle. The day and the night might be unlivable, but in the twilight in-between it was a paradise. *Your grace is plenteous, it cannot be veiled.* All they had to do to live in that paradise, Bering thought, would be to give up everything and walk—at this latitude, a mere three kilometers a day to keep up with the setting sun. Not difficult to do once, but they would have to do it every day. Forever. That meant no building houses, no farming, no village.

We'll never be in one place long enough. But you promised us a home. Haven't I shown perseverance? Haven't I sacrificed?

He considered what he had heard from pilgrims from the other four religious traditions—how they were each making sense of the situation. They had all been united in their belief in the Teacher and in the Promise that She had made, but they each understood that Promise through their own peculiar tenets and practices. The Samsarans were meditating, the Al-Mustaqimists were praying, and the Ecohumanists were debating hypotheses. Three different Samsarans he had spoken to reiterated the need to be detached, but sounding as if they themselves were anything but. In the last concourse, a Wexlerian had explained her belief that failure to heal from their collective trauma had collapsed a wave function prematurely, resulting in the illusion that the Promise had been broken. Bering heard one of the Ecohumanists, for whom all spiritual truths were emergent phenomena of complex systems, wonder aloud if the Promise had ceased to exist because now their "civilization," with a mere two hundred eighty-eight people, did not have sufficient complexity to sustain it. The Al-Mustaqimists he had engaged with, always eminently practical, had little to say about the Promise and instead were telling each other that the family just needed "to get on with it," but were unable to agree over what the "it" should be.

Two hours later, or perhaps three—he was not sure— Bering stood up, still feeling lost, and plodded back to the camp. As he neared the *Serengeti,* he saw Arsen Kazakii emerging from it carrying a large backpack apparently jammed full, his hands held out to the sides to help him balance.

When Arsen saw Bering, he quickly looked away. Then he seemed to have second thoughts, because he looked toward Bering again, waved nervously, and then kept walking, not making further eye contact.

That was just fine for Bering. He was in no mood for Arsen's incomprehensible mix of doomsaying and excited optimism. Instead, he went to find one of his engineering colleagues at the group of tents near the *Haida Gwaii* that served as their workshop. The first person he saw there was Ford Cyltemstra, sitting under a canopy, two large view screens set up in front of him, and three portable consoles beside him on a table. Now that the natural light had dimmed, a luzglobe had been hung in the canopy above him. He leaned forward in his chair, his eyes darting back and forth between two of the screens as he ate a grey vatcake.

"Bering, do you know much about excavation?"

"Just the basics, really."

"Because we don't have the materials to build our habitat above ground and construct a big, insulated dome over it. Going underground is our only option."

This was not what Bering had imagined their life on this world would look like. "So . . . We would live about seven years at a time underground, just coming out for a few months each planetary morning and evening?"

Ford tensed. "I came here to build!" he said. "No one's gonna stop me from doing that."

"Yeah, yeah. Me too."

Seeing that Bering agreed, Ford shifted from defensive back to enthusiastic. "I think if we could put most of the habitat between twenty and thirty meters deep, that would be enough to insulate us from the temperature swings. That's what I've been working on here—the calculations for all that."

Bering looked at the screens, one of which showed plans for a tunnel-boring machine. *While I'm busy feeling sorry for myself, Ford is actually doing something so that we can start to live here.* "Makes sense. We need a permanent place for our manufacturing base."

"I'm thinking that if we can reestablish contact with the ark, eventually we can also work toward orbital manufacturing, and ultimately put giant mirrors and shades in orbit to give us some heat and light at night and to reduce the worst of the heat in the day."

Ford was all enthusiasm and determination, and as much as Bering admired that, the idea sounded like something far beyond their capabilities. They had come equipped to provide for a colony with a starting population of four hundred sixty-nine people, not to build giant structures to terraform a whole world. But he held his tongue, and Ford continued expounding his ideas.

"Bering, this is the time of the human race's flowering. I believe that. This is our new home. And we *will* build a home here. That's what I came here to do."

Maybe he's got some details wrong. Maybe his exact plan isn't what will let us live here. But he has the right attitude.

Ford took his assistant from his pocket and looked at the time. "The next concourse is about to start," he said as he stood up.

"Another one?" Bering had not looked at his assistant in a while.

"I know, right? Blah, blah, blah. I don't understand why there's even any debate. Being humanity's seed is a mission we vowed to carry out with perseverance and sacrifice."

Exactly! He's putting into words what I haven't been able to. Listening to Ford was like looking into a mirror that showed him how he wanted to be.

"That's what I'm gonna tell them in the concourse," Ford continued. "We can conquer this place. We can sculpt it to our needs."

In that moment, the mirror shattered. *Conquer? Sculpt it to our needs? But we're supposed to do* better *than we did on Earth.*

He remembered the words of the prayer, "Make us worthy to recognize your gift. We will accept that gift and become part of it." In that moment, Bering saw again all the things he had seen over the past four and a half days, but now with different eyes. *This world is a gift, and we will become part of it.* He almost started to speak, to object to Ford's understanding of their mission, but then suddenly he remembered Arsen acting suspiciously a few minutes earlier and realized what the quirky ecologist was doing. He realized, too, that he had to move fast—there was no time to get into an argument to try to convince Ford.

"You go ahead," he said. "I'm going to skip this one."

"You sure? I'm sure at this one we'll finally decide to stop procrastinating and get on with the colonization plan."

"All that arguing and people not listening to each other wears me down," Bering replied truthfully.

"Suit yourself," Ford said, then walked off.

As people proceeded toward the gathering, Bering returned to the *Assiniboine*. He sat at a console and searched through the equipment library. When he did not find what he was looking for, he found images in the historical library and extrapolated 3D templates. He was not able to find everything he hoped to, but he decided he needed to limit the research to half an hour. By then, the ferry was quiet, everyone having gone to the concourse.

Bering rushed to the fabricators and loaded the templates he had created, and then as the printing began, he found a backpack and stuffed equipment into it—a sewing kit, a knife, twenty meters of rope, a change of clothes, and some food. But he made sure to not let the pack get too heavy and to leave room for the equipment that was still printing. At one point he stepped outside and looked around. There was no sign of people returning from the concourse yet, but he did not want to take any chances, so by the time ninety minutes had passed, he halted the fabricators and loaded what he had produced into the backpack.

He asked a console for the location of Arsen Kazakii.

<<Sen. Kazakii's assistant is not reachable.>>

He asked for the location of Jaykella Tahirani.

<<Frau. Tahirani's assistant is not reachable.>>

He asked for the location of Annamiek Ismail and got the same answer again.

They're already out of range. It doesn't matter—I know what direction they're going.

Bering put his backpack on his shoulders, exited the ferry, and began to walk. He looped far south of the *Serengeti* to avoid being seen by anyone at the concourse, then he turned west and kept walking. Two kilometers west of the landing sight, the valley began to gradually descend, and the terrain began to undulate. And then he spotted two parallel trails where the grass had been freshly trampled, pointing due west. He followed the trails until he came to a ridge that looked like a dune that had solidified in the process of cutting diagonally across the valley. It was about twice his height, and as he got closer, it blocked his view of the western horizon and the remaining remnant of the sun. He climbed and as he reached the crest, below him on the opposite slope was a group of pilgrims—Jaykella, Arsen, Frau Ismail, and more than a dozen others.

"That's not Gopal," someone said.

They all went quiet. Bering looked down at them from the ridge, a few of them standing, most sitting, each one of them with a backpack nearby. And every one of them stared back up at him, a few of them wide-eyed as if they had just been caught in the commission of a sin.

Or as if an uninvited guest just arrived, he thought.

He started slowly down the hill. "Can I . . . Umm . . . I mean, I'd like to come with you. I've printed a bunch of spear points like the ones you showed me that belonged to Adam, and a couple of axe heads, and some other equipment. I think maybe I—"

Jaykella jumped up and ran to him. She wrapped her arms around him, laughing as she called out his name. Then she turned back to the others. "I told you we should have invited him."

"That you did," Frau Ismail admitted, as she stood and reached for her own small backpack. "And it just wouldn't be right if the first person to open his eyes to this world wasn't with us for the start of the journey. But clearly, he figured out what we were up to anyway."

"Bering," Arsen asked, "how, man, were you knowin'—?"

"He can tell you as we walk," Frau Ismail said. "We've dithered long enough, and we have some ground to make up. Although we only need to average three kilometers a day, if we want to catch up to where we should be, we should go at least four more kilometers before we sleep, and then eight or ten tomorrow."

"But we're supposed to meet Gopal here," the tall redhead objected. "He was staying to see what got decided at the concourse."

Frau Ismail just tilted her nose up toward the ridge crest. There, coming up over the ridge right where Bering had come, was Gopal. He bent and rested his hands on his knees and caught his breath. Clearly, he had been running.

"Gopal, your backpack is here," someone called.

Gopal loped down the hill, picked up his bag, and within seconds, everyone was up and ready to continue the journey.

As they walked, Bering listened to the conversations around him, and to the strange mix of elation, humor, and sadness. Jaykella fell into step beside him and, when he caught her glance, he smiled warmly.

"We should have stolen a ground transport," someone laughed.

"You're only saying that because your pack is too heavy," another one answered. "Did you stuff a plow in there? Or just your geological samples?"

"Gopal, what news from the concourse?"

"Well, some—Wow!—some unexpected news. Not all the Earth species we're seeing were brought here 13,000 years ago. Someone captured one of those goats I saw, and when Watersmith couldn't find Arsen, he sequenced the genome himself. The goat was descended from DNA in the ark's gene library, separated by about fifty or sixty generations. So, for goats, that should be about two hundred years. That means those weren't seed ship goats I saw; they were *our* goats—or, you know, their descendants—gone feral. But not only that; Watersmith also said the goat's DNA also has some sequences from wildebeest spliced in, probably something related to migratory instincts."

"That had to be Leifson!" someone said. "He was a farming virtuoso."

"There was one other interesting bit of news at the concourse," Gopal said. "The communications team said they still haven't been able to contact the ark. But they said another beacon just started transmitting, thirty-two kilometers due west of here."

"You see! It's been two hundred years, but our brother Adam prepared things for us."

Adam, Bering thought, *and the seed ship, and the Teacher.*

"Wanna bet a third beacon further west will start transmitting in a few days?"

"The goats, and the new beacon—that must have swayed them in the concourse."

"No," Gopal answered. "They still refuse to decide."

Some of them stopped briefly once in a while to collect leaves or berries, and someone else pointed out some antelope tracks. Eventually the conversations died away, and they walked in silence, soaking in their surroundings. As they walked, the hills to the north and south became smaller, the valley floor came to an end in front of them, and they saw that they were at the top of a small escarpment. A vast, flat prairie was stretched out in front of them, and beyond that an orange, coral, and blood red sky. Four or five kilometers ahead was a herd of what Bering guessed was bison, the sun casting long shadows from the animals toward them. Awe and gratitude swept over Bering like a warm breeze, reminding him of a night as a child when, after his astronomy lessons and learning of the vastness of the Milky Way, he lay on his back in a field and let the night sky call to him. But he also realized that although the plain in front of them, and this whole world in fact, were miniscule in comparison to the expanse of the galaxy, the awe he felt now was greater, because this was life, life that spoke to his soul.

A wide path, trampled with countless hoof prints, showed them a way down the escarpment that was not very steep. As they followed it, Bering, still at Jaykella's side, spoke, "Do you think the others will follow us?"

"Leifson seems to have arranged things so that they don't really have any other choice."

And yet, he thought, *they still don't want to make that choice.* He thought about Ford and his zealous conviction in his interpretation of the Promise. And he also thought about how close he himself had come to mistaking his desires and preconceptions for his actual faith.

"I think we need to show them it can be done," he said.

Jaykella nodded. "Yes, but although Leifson seems to have left a second beacon for us, we don't know that there will be more after that, or other directions or help."

"Even if there isn't, he's already done so much for us. Either way, we'll just need to have faith and figure it out as we go."

"You know this won't be easy."

"The hardest part will be letting go of what we wanted this world to be. Instead, we need to accept the gift as it is and become part of it."

By the time they stopped to make camp, a bit more of the star's disk was visible above the horizon. They slept a while, and when they broke camp, a gentle breeze at their backs propelled them on.

The Thursday Plan

James Mfaxa fiddles with the cotton strap that encircles his neck, then touches the back of his neck to ensure once more that the jammer is still in place, directly over his spine, three finger widths below the base of his skull. He knows the pain that the implants can produce, having experienced it far more often than Johnathon has, and he is uneasy with Johnathon's decision to hold their meeting here in a house less than one hundred meters from a police station known to have a transmitter. Johnathon Themba also has an electrothalmic implant that can be triggered by the police transmitter, and although he and James are each wearing a jammer, hidden beneath the collar of a turtleneck sweater, meeting here is still risky. "Yeah, it's close to the police station," Johnathon gleefully told James and the others at their last meeting. "That's exactly why we're gonna meet there—they'd never expect us to gather right under their noses." As far as James can tell, both Ruth and Richard have accepted Johnathon's logic and seem unconcerned about where they are, but of course neither of them has an implant.

"The Thursday Plan," Johnathon says once everyone sits down. "It will happen before our next meeting."

Ruth says what she has said at other meetings: "So soon? I don't like this—it's too desperate!"

"Oh, please," moans Richard. "We've made our decision. Let's just get on with it."

"I agree it's risky," Johnathon says. "A big risk, but it's gonna be a big payoff, and the people need to see something big like this if they're gonna get their determination back. Are you against us participating?"

"Can't you find some other way?" Ruth sighs.

Richard answers her, saying what *he* has said before. "This racist regime must be punished—for Biko, for Mandela, for Tutu. Especially for Tutu."

It has only been four months since Desmond Tutu was killed after being arrested—according to their sources, tortured to death—and it is still fresh in their minds. Mandela's death in '97 was bad enough, letting an old man die alone in prison (at least they had more or less provided for his physical needs), but the government has become more bold since then, not only arresting seventy-seven-year-old Tutu, but torturing him to death.

"Ruth, are you against us participating?"

She shifts uneasily, then looks to James, who says nothing, his face expressionless. She relents with a tired whisper: "No."

"James?"

James has considered alternatives to the Thursday Plan. The steel workers' union in Johannesburg, for example, might be capable of effecting a satisfactory demonstration. Almost two dozen of the workers have the implants, and the union membership as a whole is united and courageous—a strike, an old-style strike with marching, dancing, speeches, and blockading the work site would surely provoke a response from the authorities. It would be a demonstration not only of the movement's newfound ability to jam the implants but also of its unity and resolve. James has already discussed the possibility with Johnathon, who prefers the Thursday Plan because it would be far more dramatic, because it would do more to polarize the political climate, and, James suspects, simply because it is more daring. James also prefers the Thursday Plan, but for his own reasons: he is afraid that the more their cell becomes involved in mobilizing and instigating the workers, the greater the chance that someone in the union will turn informer; he is afraid that his role as point-man in the Thursday Plan is his big chance to make his mark on history and that if he passes it up it will be gone forever; and he is afraid that if he argues against the more audacious Thursday Plan, the others will question his resolve.

An image descends unbidden into his thoughts, two sets of railroad tracks running parallel for some distance, then diverging, and he realizes that the police transmitter has been turned on. (These hallucinations only seem to happen when his jammer is engaged, screening the signals that would activate his implant.) Then, as his imaginary field of view widens, he sees that, in the other direction, other tracks have branched off from the main line at various points in the past, such as when the PAC ended all cooperation with the ANC, and when Botha died of a heart attack halfway through his second term in office. There are personal moments, as well—his decision not to marry Izzie, his decision to go to Angola for special training, and now his decision whether to support the Thursday Plan—and all of these moments are now manifested in diverging railway tracks. As the picture settles into his mind, gradually it becomes more than just a mental image; it becomes something sensory and tangible. The dark room and his three associates disappear to be replaced by a flatcar speeding along the tracks. There is another flatcar, part of another train, traveling beside him, and if he were to time it right, he could jump over to it, but only if he does so immediately, because the two sets of tracks are about to diverge. Instead, he wills the vision away.

Johnathon is repeating his question: "James, you got any objections to our cell participating in the Plan?"

"None. Let's get on with it."

* * *

Sunday morning, less than five days before the execution of the plan, James is surprised to find a man at his door. He is tall, perhaps in his early forties, and wearing the new unofficial uniform of the anti-apartheid resistance: a turtleneck sweater.

"James Mfaxa?"

"Yes."

"I would like to speak with you. May I come in?"

"Who are you?"

"Luke Tshatshu."

Immediately, James' heart is racing. He knows the name, knows it very well, but the security protocol is that he is never to meet Luke Tshatshu—unless something goes wrong. His first thought is that something has happened to Johnathon. Luke Tshatshu, not his real name of course, is from two levels above him in the organization, the captain of Johnathon's cell just as Johnathon is the captain of James' cell. Luke Tshatshu has been, until now, nothing more than a faceless series of directives conveyed through Johnathon.

If this actually is Luke Tshatshu—the stranger has provided no proof. But then he gives it.

"I met your sister in London."

James has no sister. This is the code that Jonathan taught him. He invites the stranger in.

"Are we alone?"

"My sister and her children have gone out—we're alone. What's happened to Johnathon? Is he hurt? Arrested? What's going on?"

"No, nothing like that. But we're..." The stranger pauses, searching for a word. "... concerned. Concerned about Johnathon. There's some indication that he's become a free agent, planning his own radical measures without the knowledge of the organization. Unfortunately, the nature of this sort of compartmentalized organizational set-up makes such a thing very possible: you, for example, have no choice but to trust that Johnathon is working in conformity with the wishes and plans of the organization and of those above him; in the same way, he has no choice but to trust that I am."

Until now, it has not even crossed James' mind that the Thursday Plan might not have been sanctioned by the organization, but he knows Johnathon and is not really surprised. Johnathon is committed, determined, and passionate, but he also loves the thrill, the kind of thrill that would accompany the execution of something so grand, so dangerous, against not only the defenses of the government but also the wishes of the organization. The only real surprise is the scale of Johnathon's temerity.

"So, what is it that you think he's planning to do?" James asks.

"Well," says the stranger, sitting down, "why don't *you* tell *me* what your cell has been working on?"

In a way, James admires Johnathon's audacity, but he realizes, as well, the precariousness of the situation. Johnathon is potentially in a great deal of trouble. He suspects that he is quite likely in just as much trouble himself, along with Ruth and Richard, but what frightens him even more deeply is knowing that the Thursday Plan is in jeopardy.

"We've been working with a few trade unions and student groups," he says, "looking, you know, for an opportunity to demonstrate the jammers." He lurches uncertainly to the old computer desk in the corner, opens a drawer, and pulls out the little plastic box attached to a black, cotton strap. "Ever seen one of these?"

The stranger smiles and pats the back of his neck. "I know them very well." Then, hearing screaming from outside, somewhere down the street, he turns his head toward the window.

"It's not what you'd call a peaceful life here in the townships," says James, laughing nervously. He takes a breath. "So, you have a jammer?"

Turning back, the stranger nods. "I was sentenced to 'preventative electrothalmic probation' three months ago. They're resorting to implants more and more, I'm afraid."

The South African government began using the implants in twenty-oh-five; by now, three years later, over four hundred activists have received them. Based on very simple electronics and very complex European nerve regeneration technology, the implant is wired directly into the central nervous system, in particular, the pain centers in the thalamus, and is activated by signals on any one of several different radio frequencies. Once activated, it will produce one of two effects: excruciating pain or uncon- sciousness. Each implant is also booby-trapped against tampering or removal with a lethal dose of poison. Different poisons are used and, of course, the recipient is not told which poison his implant contains. It is not impossible for a sympathetic surgeon who knows what he is doing to remove the implant safely, but such surgeons are rare.

A person with an implant can also protect himself by staying at least one kilometer away from any police transmitter, but this amounts to defense by compliance, so until now the implants have been effective. Nevertheless, change seems to be on the horizon: the jammers, which were developed last year by an Angolan engineering student, have so far proven to be 100% effective.

"What were you saying about a demonstration?" the stranger asks.

"Oh, right. So, anyway, we've been trying to assess, you know, which group actually has the capacity to pull it off. So far, the answer is none of them, but we're trying to help the groups to develop and mature."

"And has your cell been working on anything else? Anything related to your special skills or Richard's?"

James tries, with little success, to calm himself, not knowing what to do. In fabricating a major scheme like the Thursday Plan outside of the organization's proper channels, Johnathon has deceived and endangered his subordinates, Ruth, Richard, and James. At the same time, James does not want to abandon the Thursday Plan and what it represents to him, fearing that if he loses it, he will lose the last source of purpose in his life. In his thoughts, he fires a prayer like a signal flare into the sky, begging someone or something for guidance and clarity. As he does, he notes without time for a second thought that the distant screaming they have been hearing has still not stopped.

"So, are you saying," James asks, "that you think Johnathon is involved in some sort of sabotage operat—"

Suddenly, he feels bolts of agony searing through every fiber of his body, and every muscle tenses, fighting against every other muscle. Finding himself on the ground, he tries to somehow crawl away from the pain, but is unable to coordinate his arms and legs. He realizes that the police must be nearby with a mobile transmitter, but he is unable to form any other coherent thoughts, and then, without any sort of transition, he is detached from his body. The pain is still there, still extreme, but it now seems slightly less immediate and relevant. Looking back to his body, he sees two—two bodies in two very different worlds. One world he knows very well for he has lived it, but beyond it his other self is neither screaming nor writhing on the floor. As he begins to access his memories from this alternate world, he sees that it is a saner place in which apartheid is more than a decade dead. He tries to approach it but is blocked by a solid wall of pain. And the pain continues, until. . .

He feels the stranger, "Luke Tshatshu", pressing the jammer against the back of his neck. Suddenly the pain, along with any perceptions that remained of the two realities, disappears, replaced by a more abstract hallucination of the kind he is familiar with. The two realities collapse into two slits in a card toward which he has been cast like a beam of light in a secondary school physics experiment. Were he merely a beam of light, he would simply pass through the two slits to the other side. Even a single electron would somehow find a way to pass through both slits. But he is a mortal being, and he knows that by Thursday, at the latest, he must choose.

* * *

"Bloody hell!" says Richard peeking through the curtains down to the street. "What the hell are those protesters doing there?"

James, pretending to be concerned, comes to the hotel room window to look down to the street with Richard, where police are strung across the road blocking a group of about forty people, a few carrying drums, the rest placards. James, turning his back on Richard, nods to himself—the student activists have positioned themselves perfectly, and he knows well enough the way the police will handle a situation like this. They will assume that at least some of the protesters have implants, which they do, and with the president so close, they will undoubtedly have a mobile transmitter nearby. James only hopes that the police will not have finished using it before the President emerges from the building sixty meters down the street where he is addressing the local Chamber of Commerce.

"Never mind," he tells Richard. "We will just, you know, have to make the best of it. Close the curtains."

Richard steps away from the window and goes to sit beside the door, a pistol in his hand. His job is to keep watch and to protect James. "Are you wearing your jammer? It looks as if you'll need it."

James pulls down the front of his turtleneck to reveal the cotton strap that circles his neck just below his Adam's apple. Then he pulls it back up, sits down on the bed, and opens the suitcase that he has been carrying. Inside are a pair of binoculars, two sandwiches, a pair of gloves, the rifle and its scope, and three magazines of ammunition. He tosses a sandwich to Richard, puts on the gloves, then begins to assemble the Steyr-Mannlicher SSG-69, the same rifle he trained with in Angola. Once assembled, he sets it beside the window, opens the curtains a sliver, and then checks his line of sight: completely unobstructed. He glances at his watch. It is 3:49, and if their information is correct, the president will emerge from the building any time between 3:54 and 4:09. James picks up the binoculars and begins to watch.

He has been watching for seven minutes when he hears a quick succession of sounds from the street below: vehicles pulling up, shouts, and then screams from several different voices. He pulls the binoculars away and briefly looks down, seeing that police reinforcements have arrived to deal with the protesters.

"What is it?" Richard asks, getting up from his chair and moving toward the window.

"Stay by the door," James commands as he puts the binoculars back up to his eyes. "It's only the police. It looks as if some of those protesters have implants."

"The police are using a transmitter?" Richard asks, returning to his seat. "Oh, my friend, you must be glad for that jammer you're wearing!"

"If I didn't have it, I would be trying to jump out this window just to end—"

James stops in mid-sentence, throwing the binoculars on the bed and quickly taking up the rifle. He tucks the butt against his shoulder and tilts his head slightly, peering through the scope with his right eye. It only takes him half a second to sight on the first of the men that have emerged from the building: bodyguards. He tries to calm himself, to stop his heart from pounding in his ears, but his uncertainty about what he will do next makes this impossible. Everything seems to be happening with perfect timing, just as he has planned: they have successfully kept the plan secret from Luke Tshatshu, he and Richard are in the hotel room, and the police transmitter is broadcasting, sending the signal to activate any implants in the area. And, most importantly, his jammer is on, transforming the signal and co-opting his implant to create, instead of pain, choices.

Yet, as he sights on the next man and the next, he realizes that part of him still doubts the visions he has had, wonders if they have been merely the hallucinations of a madman who was driven insane by three days of police torture when his implant was first installed. Part of him is still terrified at the idea of not going through with the Thursday Plan, of having to accept that his two years of planning and training for this day have been a sterile, vain lie. And part of him is terrified that the real reason he is searching for a way to not go through with the Plan is that, after two decades of actively fighting apartheid, he has finally discovered the limit of his commitment and resolve. Yet despite the doubts and the fears, even as President Groenewald comes into his sights, James can feel, deep in his soul, that this is unnecessary, counter-productive, and wrong, and that having the steel workers' union in Johannesburg go on strike to demonstrate to a wary and demoralized populace the efficacy of the jammers and the ability of united people to defy the oppressors is a better way.

And then it happens. He can feel it, spreading quickly from the implant at the back of his skull to all parts of his mind—one of his hallucinations—and he briefly feels some sense of relief. He sees himself as a bird, flying beside a tall cliff, high, high above a rocky plain, unable to find an updraft. With his mind's eye he observes the scene solidifying and becoming more and more tangible, but he knows that he must focus on the reality frozen in time around him and make a decision. The mental image that he is a tired bird, as it becomes more palpable, supplanting the hotel room and the street and the magnified image of the president in his telescopic sight, does not distract him from the choice that he has before him; instead, the vision—for it is no longer just a mental image—seems to make the choice more immediate and real. He wants to keep flapping his wings, but he is exhausted, and all he must do to relieve the pain in his muscles is let himself pull the trigger. There is no perch on which to rest: he must climb or drop.

Somehow, he is able to see the plateau above him, and compared to the rocky plain below it is a world of surpassing beauty, yet beyond it, majestic falcons are ascending to even higher plateaus. So, with an effort of will, James beats his wings, removes his finger from the trigger, and flies up to another universe.

"James, what are you doing? James—"

As the rifle evaporates into wisps of memory and the telescopic sight becomes a television on the other side of the evolving room, he watches President Groenewald transform into a different man, a black man whose face he knows—one of the ANC leaders. James begins to remember this new universe, how Tutu did not die in prison, nor Mandela, how apartheid was brought down in '94, how the nation has struggled since then to foster healing, justice, and prosperity, and how he has been active in that struggle.

"James!"

He looks over and sees that Richard is still with him, but now accompanied by Johnathon and Ruth, all of them sitting at a table, waiting for him.

"He's not saying anything new," says Richard, pointing to President Mbeki on the television. "Put it off."

"The stay-at-home," Johnathon says, once James joins them at the table. "We must decide about it now."

"A stay-at-home?" Richard objects. "A general strike? A bit desperate, don't you think?"

Ruth leans forward. "These austerity measures have to be stopped. The government has lost touch and doesn't understand that it's the poor who are bearing the weight of these reductions."

Out of habit, James reaches behind his neck to fiddle with his jammer but finds that it is not there. He is not even wearing a turtleneck sweater. Then he remembers that in this universe there have never been implants, and he smiles. As he remembers more about who he is and what he has been fighting for, he realizes that he has some difficult decisions ahead of him. But with no implant and no jammer, how will he know what to choose? As Johnathon asks for his opinion, he mutters a prayer for clarity, trying to envision the type of world he would like to create.

Problem Solving

Demba Kebba Darbo was unemployed and sitting in his favorite drinking establishment when he realized that what he had always thought was his bad luck was actually bad timing. He filed the realization in his brain under *I* for "Irrelevant". It was like realizing that you had missed your bus by five minutes instead of by ten.

D.K., as his friends called him, had been at a table in the corner of this bar, facing the wall, all afternoon. Finally, he stood up, began placing the notes for a short story he was writing into a ragged briefcase, and called to his friend the bartender. "I have to catch the bus to Serrekunda," he said. D.K. turned toward the door, but jumped back in surprise when he saw an alien sitting on a stool at the bar counter. He had never seen one up close. It looked somewhat like Queen Victoria when she had been old and fat, except that it was pinker, it was fatter, and it had at least fourteen short tentacles sprouting from its upper body instead of two arms. It was also naked, unlike ninety percent of the paintings and statues of Queen Victoria that I've seen.

Bakary, the bartender, had been serving aliens on occasion for two weeks by this time. He chuckled at D.K.'s reaction, then said, "Your bus left ten minutes ago."

"No, I tthhink fffiveff," the alien objected.

D.K. trudged to the bar counter and slumped into his usual stool, which was two to the left of the alien's. He pulled his unopened mail out of the briefcase. Two of the three envelopes he recognized as coming from companies where he had applied for jobs. He opened the third. As he read it, he deflated like a slowly leaking balloon and sighed, "Bloody hell!"

"Bad news?" Bakary the sympathetic bartender asked.

"It's a rejection letter from *Stupendous Science Fiction* in Kenya," D.K. answered.

"Why are they rejecting your story?"

"It's a form letter with one handwritten sentence fragment at the bottom. It says, 'Competently handled, but will find it easier to sell a story with problem-solving characters.'" D.K. crumpled the letter and whined, "I don't want to write about people who solve problems. I want to write about despair and hopelessness."

"Do you get a lot offf rejectthun letterth?" the alien lisped.

D.K. eyed the alien uneasily. "Scads." But he wanted to be friendly, so he relaxed and recounted a story. "There was one letter from about two years ago that I remember clearly. I had just risked imprisonment to exchange every African franc I had for U.S. dollars on the black market—I had a business idea. One hour after exchanging the currency, we heard the news that Brazil, Argentina and Mexico had simultaneously announced they were bankrupt and were defaulting on all foreign debts. The world economy collapsed and the American currency suddenly became worthless. I was wiped out."

"Bad timing," said Bakary.

D.K. thought about that. The seemingly innocuous statement was actually a very profound and accurate description of his life's misfortunes. "I think you're right," he said to Bakary. "I had always thought it was bad luck, but I think it *is* bad timing."

"What doeth that havff to do with the rejecthun letter?" asked the alien.

"Ah, yes. I received it three weeks later. It was for a story I had written about the collapse of First World economies and societies that occurs after several Third World nations default on their debts. I had submitted the story *six weeks BEFORE* the Latin American announcement."

D.K. paused to let that sink in.

"The rejection letter read, 'Your story may have been SF when you wrote it, but it isn't now.' They didn't even bother to return the manuscript."

Bakary the bartender sympathetically poured D.K. a drink.

"We havff a word fffor that thort of bad timing—" said the alien, "*paathyldyeff*. You theem to havfff negativfff paathyldyeff."

Okay, thought D.K., *I have bad timing, or paathyldyeff, instead of bad luck. So what?* It was like learning that your crops had been destroyed by locusts instead of by disease.

D.K. summed up his problems: "I have bad timing, I cannot make a living as a writer, I'm unemployed, and I missed my bus by five minutes."

"Ten," said Bakary.

"Do not worry," the alien advised. "Now that Earth ith a member of our federaython, itth economy will improvff and you will get a job."

D.K. ignored this attempt to comfort him. He guessed that his whole life had been happening about two and one half months late.

* * *

Two and one half months later, D.K. thought of something he should have asked the alien: "What if we don't want to be in your federation?"

But it was too late, and anyhow, his train of thought was interrupted as he opened a letter. The letter said he was being offered a job in the Senegambian civil service. That afternoon, he went to the mosque, apologized to Allah for not having quit drinking and thanked Him for his good fortune. Then he went to the bar.

"Bakary! Bakary! Where are you?"

"I'm back here," Bakary's calm, melodic voice replied.

D.K. scurried over to his regular stool and looked over the counter. Bakary was sitting on the floor behind it looking very contented. A chrome scorpion-like thing was latched onto the top of his head. Neon-green letters were emblazoned on the back of the "scorpion". D.K. could not read them because they were alien letters, but he knew they spelled "Zilco".

"What are you doing?" D.K. demanded.

"Enjoying," Bakary sighed as he marveled at the spots in his thumbnail.

"Take that off—you're drunk!" D.K. reached over the bar and snatched the Pleasure Centre Stimulator, made by Zilco Interstellar Limited, from Bakary's head. Bakary's smile faded. "It's a good thing the aliens are leaving tonight!" D.K. exclaimed. (Bakary's lower lip began to tremble.) "I know more ships will come—this was just the first, but look what it's done already." (Bakary sniffled.)

"And not only these addictive PCSes, but just at the moment that the world economy is becoming fair and just, they give us plants that they want us to grow as cash crops." (A tear trickled down Bakary's left cheek.) "They've promised to lend us interstellar federation money because we are so 'backward'. It's the World Bank and USAID all over again!"

D.K. would have ranted further, but at that point two aliens burst into the bar. One of them held a pointy steel rod in one of its tentacles. It pointed this pointy rod at D.K. The other one said, "You will come withth uth to the mother thip."

"B-b-but you're l-l-leaving tonight," D.K. stuttered.

"Yeth. You will be leavfing Earthth. No more quethtionth!"

"W-w-wait! Isn't th-th-there anything I c-c-can do?"

"Are you mocking my pronunthiathon?"

"N-n-no!"

"I thertainly hope not." Then the alien pondered. "But perhaps there ith thomething you can do. Give uth one million franch and we will thay that we could not fffind you."

D.K. stopped stuttering and yelled. "One million francs! It would take me two and a half months at my new job to save that much!"

"Iff you do not have it you will come now."

"Wait! Let me pay in instalments."

"Ath you already thaid, we are leavfing tonight."

D.K. decided that there was nothing he could do. He sighed, "So if I had saved up from my job for two and a half months and if I had found that job two and a half months ago instead of today, I would be able to stay on Earth? As simple as that?"

From behind the bar Bakary whimpered, "Bad timing, D.K."

* * *

D.K. was sure that he had been taken prisoner because of his nasty remarks about the aliens, their federation, and their gadgets, but once he was aboard the mother ship, he learned the truth. He was presented to an alien who looked a little more like Queen Victoria and whose lisp was a little worse than the other aliens. This alien told D.K. that he was being taken from Earth because he had the highly valued gift of paathyldyeff, or "bad timing" as he imprecisely referred to it. The alien also told D.K. that the ship's paathyldyeffkin would teach him to control his paathyldyeff and that once they reached the federation capital, he would become very wealthy. D.K. had trouble believing this.

"What's in it for you?" he asked.

"I will altho become wealthy and probably famouth when I tell them that not only havff I found a paathyldyeffkin, but I havff dithcovfered a new intelligent thpecieth."

"The federation doesn't know about Earth yet? Didn't you radio them?"

"Radio wayvth would take hundredth of yearth to make the trip. We will travfel through Zilco-thpayth and be there in two."

D.K. wondered why the alien could pronounce the *z* in *Zilco* but not in any other words. But he did not let this question bother him. It was like wondering whether your dysentery was being caused by an amoebic infection or a bacterial infection when you didn't have medicine for either.

D.K. spent about half his free time receiving lessons from the ship's paathyldyeffkin. He (it?) instructed D.K. that federation science knew of only one form of time travel, which could only be performed by paathyldyef-fkin. Paathyldyeffkin were beings who performed actions that were displaced from their proper location in the space-time continuum. These actions could be performed either later than their correct location in the continuum (negative paathyldyeff) or earlier than their correct location in the continuum (positive paathyldyeff).

Included in the lessons was time for experimenting in the Zilco Paathyldyeff Adjustment Chamber.

"This chamber is supposed to change my bad timing into good timing?" he asked his mentor incredulously.

"I do not know why you inthitht on putting a value judgment on paathyldyeff. There ith no good or bad paathyldyeff. In the Paathyldyeff Adjuthtment Chamber you can alter your time dithplathement pothitivffly or negativffly."

After several months of experimenting, D.K. had not yet noticed any such effects. This was why he spent only half of his spare time paathyldyeffing. The other half, he spent writing. The alien that looked a little more like Queen Victoria than the others had told him that the federation did indeed have science fiction literature and that it read a lot of it. D.K. gave one story to the alien to hear its criticism. The alien invited him to the ship's bridge.

"Ah, Mithter Darbo, welcome to the bridge. I hope your amoebic dythentery problem hath cleared up."

"Hmm? Oh, yes."

D.K. was awed by the bridge. There were hundreds of gadgets and blinking lights and display screens all beyond his comprehension. There were small Zilco Ltd. robots scurrying across the floor, electronic arcs zapping through the air between metal doodads, and smoking, bubbling liquids with wires dipped into them.

The Queen Victoriaest alien waited for D.K. to get over his awe. He didn't. "Ahem, well, your thtory," the alien finally said. "I found your Earth verthion of thienth ficthon ffery interethting. You are deffinitely a competent writer. However, the dethpair and thynithism of your protagonitht ith thomewhat unappealing. You thould try writing thtorieth baytht on characterth with enoufff get-up-and-go to tholve problemth."

"Solve problems! Arrgh!" screamed D.K. "Doesn't anyone in the universe know how disgusting the universe is?"

He whirled around so he could stomp away angrily, but on his second stomp he violently upset a bucket of smoking, bubbling liquid. It splashed onto a gadget with flashing lights and lots of wires attached to it. The liquid seeped into the gadget and down into the floor. Suddenly there was chaos. The lights went out as if someone had forgotten to pay the electricity bill. Machines started buzzing, then emergency lights came on, and then there were fat, naked, tentacled Queen Victorias running in every direction. D.K. fled and hid.

Ten minutes later, the head alien found D.K. Very calmly and quietly it said, "Hiding in the thuttle thip docking thecthon will do you no good."

"Shuttle ship docking? Oh, is that where I am?"

"Yeth. Now, do you know what you'vff done?"

"Not precisely."

"You havff thpilled liquid nitrogen on our navigathon computer. The damage wath only parthial but the knowledge of our dethtinaython and of the locathon of all ffederaython planetth thath the thip could pothibly reach hath been dethroyed. We will either havff to return to Earth or go to the hibernaython tankth and drift aimlethly hoping that thomeone will rethcue uth." For emphasis, the alien said its next sentence very slowly. "You will thuffer, Mithter Darbo."

The alien was interrupted by another alien that had arrived on the scene—the paathyldyeffkin. "That won't be nethethary," it boomed heroically. "We have been rethcued already."

The head alien said something in alienish.

The paathyldyeffkin continued to speak in English for D.K.'s benefit. "Itth true, we have been rethcued by a pathing thupply thip. They are repairing our computer at thith moment. It theemth that their captain is a paathyldyeffkin and his paathyldyeff was adjuthted to thero. You thee, Mithter Darbo—iff you learn to control your paathyldyeff you can be in the right plathe at the right time."

D.K. smiled meekly and slunk away. He went to the Zilco PAC and entered it. "Chamber," he said, "give me a reading on my current paathyldyeff adjustment in Earth units."

A female voice (with no lisp) responded, "Paathyldyeff is currently set at positive six weeks, two days, three hours, and thirty-two minutes."

This confused D.K. It meant that the correct space-time location of his actions, including the act of spilling liquid nitrogen in the bridge, would be six weeks, two days, three hours, and thirty-one minutes later. *Maybe if I had spilled it then, I wouldn't have gotten into trouble*, he speculated. But he did not let it bother him. It was like wondering if the United States and IMF should have given debt relief to the Third World. It was all nitrogen under the bridge.

* * *

Two weeks later, however, this paathyldyeff problem started to bother D.K. again. A week after that, he realized what he had to do. D.K. changed his entire pattern of activities. After setting his paathyldyeff at zero, he quit attending the lessons. Then he asked to be taught the minimum he needed to know to fly a shuttle ship. An alien pilot was glad to oblige, as there was nothing D.K. could do with the information. D.K. also asked to borrow some hibernation equipment. A doctor was glad to oblige. And he borrowed someone's Zilco Super Duper Pleasure Centre Stimulator — the latest model.

He gave the Queen Victoriaest alien another of his stories to critique. The alien invited D.K. to come to the bridge the following day. D.K. calculated. If he showed up on time, he would be on the bridge exactly six weeks, two days, three hours, and thirty-one minutes later than the last time, when he had caused all the trouble. Then he asked an officer who worked on the bridge to copy some information from the navigational computer onto a portable computer data nodule: a star map, including the position of Earth, and all Zilco-space routes between their position and Earth. The officer was glad to help D.K. learn more about the science of navigation.

When D.K. went to the bridge the next morning, he carried a sack containing the Zilco Super Duper PCS, the portable data nodule, the necessary drugs and gadgets to induce hibernation, and the best short story he had written in the past seven months on the ship.

"Ah, Mithter Darbo, welcome to the bridge. I hope your amoebic dythentery problem hath cleared up."

"Bacterial dysentery, actually, but yes, it has. More than six weeks ago." D.K. pretended to examine the bridge in awe.

"Ahem, well, your thtory," the alien finally said. "I'm afffraid I found thith thtory much like the latht one. Thienth ficthon readerth havff activff, thientiffic mindth. They like to be challenged. You really thould try writing about problem-tholving characterth."

D.K. leaned forward and asked, "Did you pass on the data about your discovery of Earth to the supply ship that rescued us slightly less than six weeks, two days, three hours, and thirty-one minutes ago?"

"No, but what—"

"Problem-solving characters?"

The head alien was confused. "Yeth! But why did you athk—"

"Arrgh!" screamed D.K. in mock anger. "Problem-solving characters! Doesn't anyone in the universe know how disgusting the universe is?"

He whirled around as if about to stomp away angrily, but on his second stomp he violently upset a bucket of smoking, bubbling liquid. It splashed onto the Zilco navigational computer. Chaos ensued, much as before, and D.K. ran to the shuttle ship docking section, much as before. This time, however, he did not hide, but entered a docked shuttle ship. He pressed a button and said, "Computer, tie into mother ship's navigational computer. Give me the location of the recently discovered planet known as Earth."

The computer replied, "No recent discoveries or planets by that name registered. Systems error. Zilco navigational computer malfunctioning. Memory banks seven, nine, and—"

"Okay, okay. Just checking. Can you retrace our Zilco-space route for the previous seven months?"

"No such data available. Systems error. Zilco navi—"

"Okay! Disconnect link to mother ship computer." D.K. smiled, slotted the portable data nodule, and said, "Computer, plot a course to recently discovered planet known as Earth. Data accessible through data port number one. Then disengage from mother ship. Then fly course on automatic."

As the shuttle ship began moving, D.K. attached the hibernation gadgets to himself, set the duration to just under seven months, and administered the necessary drugs.

When D.K. woke up, he instructed the shuttle ship to land, not in Senegambia but in downtown Nairobi, Kenya. When it landed, he got out and began looking for the office of *Stupendous Science Fiction*. He found it. He reached into his sack and handed his story to the editor.

"I am submitting this story for publication. I will be back tomorrow."

He came back the next morning.

"Ah, Mr. Darbo. Good to see you. You know, most writers do not come in person. Well, to your story. You are definitely a competent writer. The problem is the basis of your plot. You see, most science fiction readers like to read stories about problem-solving—"

D.K. reached into his sack, then slapped the Zilco Super Duper Pleasure Centre Stimulator onto the editor's head. The editor's face suddenly took on an angelic quality. "Actually," she said, her voice now much more smooth and musical, "I like to read about despair and hopelessness, and we have been looking for something to fill a gap in next month's issue. I'm glad you submitted this. Good timing."

"I know," said D.K. "I know."

Communion

Matthew Rogers hated being caught away from his colony during solar flare activity. Back at Lagrangia he would have been able to wander anywhere in the colony—its hull was thick and radiation safe. Here at U.N. Station Unity, however, solar flares meant staying in specially designed compartments. To make things worse, more than a hundred statesmen, diplomats, and their staff were visiting Unity for the summit talks. The presence of these extra bodies had transformed the shielded rooms into a series of sardine cans. The summit, which this flare activity had delayed, was unprecedented. The leaders of all eight colonies were meeting to find a way to stop the world's escalating violence from cracking their fragile peace. The summit had attracted the attention of politicians, journalists, generals, terrorists, everyone.

Luckily, the radiation dropped to a safe level in only three days. Soon Matthew and several other workers would be outside the station in pressure suits checking spaceships and doing routine maintenance for Unity, while the summit went on inside. But it was Sunday, and

Matthew decided to attend a worship service before he went out to work—he felt guilty about not having been to church in a while. This was an interdenominational, Christian service conducted by a minister who was part of the Unity crew. The crew of Unity was international, so Jewish and Muslim services were also conducted. The hall was packed, but many chairs remained unoccupied while visiting politicians milled about shaking hands. As Matt understood it, their meetings would deal with two main problems: the increasing militarization of space by the superpowers and the use of American facilities by private corporations, which many colonists feared gave terrorists and extremist governments a chance to operate in space.

Looking around, Matt spotted Ismail Iqbal, who had trained with him in flight school. Ismail had later moved from Lagrangia, Matthew's home and the first colony that the United States built, to Stanford, which was more independent. Like Matt, he had flown his colony leaders to the summit meeting.

Why is he attending this service? Matt wondered. They'll have Muslim prayers here, later. Ismail was devout and always vocal about his religion. Matt could not stand him. Then he realized the answer to his question. All the visitors from Stanford—government officials, secretaries, and ship crew—were standing together, using the pre-worship socializing as an opportunity for a show of Stanford's solidarity. "P.R.," Matt whispered in disgust. As the organ prelude began, the worshippers went to sit down and Ismail made a discreet exit.

Matthew was a religious man, but he found it difficult to remain attentive during the service that morning. While the minister gave his sermon, Matt skimmed through a pamphlet he had picked up from the floor. It discussed the Eucharist.

"Bread: Christ's body broken for us. Wine: Christ's blood which seals the new covenant…

"Five aspects of the Eucharist. One: thanksgiving to the Father…. The Eucharist is the great sacrifice of praise…

"Two: memorial of Christ.—'Do this in memory of me.'…

"Three: communion…"

Matt put down the pamphlet, wondering that Ismail had even come near a Christian worship service. He's probably trying to kiss up to his superiors by going along with their "united-front church visit". Then Matt recognized his emotions: distrust, hate, jealousy. The main reason Ismail repelled him, he knew, was that he had gotten higher grades than him in flight and maintenance training. Hearing the minister's voice made Matthew's guilt more acute, and he reminded himself of other sins.

As everyone stood for a hymn, he considered the nonexistent work hours he had claimed and been paid for. And he remembered his rudeness to others during the past three days of isolation. He felt inadequate. He sinned gratuitously and often enjoyed it. He was not worthy of God's grace. Then with a start, Matt realized that the church service was finished. He hurried to one of the four "spokes" and waited for an elevator, not speaking to or looking at anyone.

Unity, like most permanent space stations, was wheel-shaped and spinning to provide artificial gravity. He ascended in the elevator toward the hub, going from one half Earth-normal gravity into nearly complete weightlessness. Barb Watson, who had co-piloted the flight from Lagrangia with him, was waiting there with the assistant they had asked for.

"Matt, this is Liem Tsu. He's stationed here at Unity and he'll be helping us."

"Hello," said Matt.

"How do you do?" There was silence as Matthew said nothing. "Shall we go?" Liem finally suggested.

Barb led the way through a stem which extended from the station's hub along the axis of rotation. They pulled themselves by the ladder, travelling head first, toward the ship docking bays at the other end of the stem. Matthew and Barb had their pressure suits waiting in the ship; Liem carried his suit with him. Matt started to tell Liem what tools they would need, but Liem was having some trouble handling his suit. Matt and Barb waited as he captured a glove which had floated away from him.

When they reached the docking bay, Matt asked Liem to get the tools and meet them outside. "Do you think you can handle that?" Matt asked sarcastically.

"What kind of training does he have?" he asked Barb a minute later, as they crawled through a small tunnel into their ferry.

"He has the primary space-systems maintenance training and a master's degree in rocketry engineering from UCLA."

Matt's acrimony was quickly replaced by guilt, again. He had treated Liem Tsu badly, never suspecting that he would have anything near a master's degree.

Matt and Barb began to don the pressure suits. They stayed in separate compartments of the ship while they removed their casual clothes and put on the water-cooled underwear of the pressure suit, then they helped each other with the outer garment. Even though the liquid-cooled, grey long johns with their web of plastic tubing was not very attractive, Matthew could not help noticing how Barb's lower back curved and the flare of her hips.

Then he reminded himself that she was married. Guilt again.

Matt tucked a nourishment bar into the cavity at the chin of his helmet and made sure he had enough drinking water. And when, after a few minutes, the helmets and gloves were on, he and Barb checked that their suits were functioning properly. Water was circulating and being cooled. Radios worked. Oxygen pressure good. Waste gasses being absorbed. They put down their helmet visors and went outside. Barb tethered herself to a rail on the outside of the ship and helped Matt to strap the jetpack to his back. Barb and Liem would not need to be moving around, so only Matt had the "manned maneuvering unit." (Everyone just called it a jetpack.) On the way to Unity they had had trouble with the radiator panels of their ship, and on the other side of the docking bay there were some new ones ready and waiting for him. Matt would replace the old ones so they could be inspected and repaired carefully. He fired the oxygen jets and flew off to get the spare parts. Originally jetpacks had used nitrogen as a propellant but lunar mining had made oxygen the cheapest gas anywhere off the Earth.

Matthew looked around. He could see the Earth and recognized two constellations: the Southern Cross and Scorpio. The moon was hidden from sight behind the docking bay. He hadn't been "outside," as space dwellers referred to the vacuum of outer space, for two weeks. The eight space colonies each had parks and ponds and birds and fresh air, but that was all still inside. There were always walls, a floor, and a ceiling holding the air in. Only here, fully exposed to the cosmic rays, the sun's ultraviolet radiation, and total vacuum could Matthew be said to be "outside". He had been outside dozens of times, but still once in a while he thought about the emptiness of space and would shiver with anxiety. In almost any direction he could point, he knew, there was nothing but occasional hydrogen atoms. But it still felt good to be outside after being squashed in that shielded room for three days.

Matt looked at the ships radiating out from the spherical docking bay, and the crews buzzing around them. There appeared to be nine "ferry" class ships, two "tugs," and one shuttle plane. From a greater distance, he knew, the docking bay would look like a flower, with the ships as petals. Matthew had seen a dozen paintings of such structures. But these thoughts were cut short when he and all the others outside in pressure suits heard a startling announcement on the common emergency frequency. "Attention all crew members. We may be in danger of a terrorist bomb strike. Please suspend all maintenance and repair operations and return to the station. I repeat. There is a possibility of a terrorist bomb aboard the station. Please suspend all EVAs."

Already Matt could see the crews scurrying around. "Barb, you go on in. It'll take me a minute to get back there."

"Hey you!" an excited voice called, apparently having switched his transmissions to the common emergency frequency. "You with the jetpack, come in over here. It's closer."

Matt saw whose voice it must have been. He was down at an airlock, hanging on to a handrail, in the shadow of the docking bay. Matt rotated until he was facing the airlock and applied a bit of thrust. Just as Matt's jets brought him to the airlock, the other fellow flipped the emergency entry lever—an override mechanism required because of safety regulations. Apparently, he did not want to waste time waiting for the air to be sucked from the room. The doors jerked open and the air rushed out. This airlock was a large room with a small door, so anything loose near the door when it was opened would be swept out with the rushing air. A pressure suit helmet and then the astronaut it belonged to were among the debris that was blown into space when the door was opened. The man who had called Matt had not checked to see if anyone was inside the airlock.

Matt recognized Liem Tsu as the one who had been in the airlock. His helmet was the only thing that he had left to put on. Matt saw Liem grasp for it. But the helmet was out of reach and moving farther away. Matt thought he could see the moisture from Liem's final exhaled breath crystallizing on his face. Matt shivered, knowing that the heat must have been rushing from Liem's body. He tried to aim himself in Liem's direction, but the tools that Liem had been bringing had been blown out of the airlock, too, and were getting in the way. Liem could stay conscious for no more than a few more seconds.

Matt applied thrust and started moving toward Liem. But then Liem threw a small arc-welder from his belt at him. Then he threw another tool and another. Liem was trying to propel himself toward his helmet by flinging mass in the opposite direction, but he had made Matt the target of the flying tools, in the meantime. Matt had to dodge the flying tools and this was slowing him down. If only he could call Liem on the radio. But of course, he couldn't: the radio was in Liem's helmet. He gained on Liem and Liem had gained on the helmet. Now it was just out of his reach. Suddenly it shone with reflected light. Matt did not understand. Was someone helping them by shining a spotlight? He did not realize that they were leaving the shadow of the docking bay. Liem was only half a second behind his helmet in leaving the shadow, and he looked directly at the sun. The sun, not screened by an atmosphere or a helmet's visor, burned into his eyes. Liem cringed and tried to hide his head, and Matt knew that he was trying to scream. Then Liem stopped moving.

In a few seconds, Matt was able to grab Liem. Then he reached the helmet and slammed it onto Liem's head. Slamming was a mistake, because it sent Matt spinning in the opposite direction. He calmed down, and clipped the helmet into place, then checked to see that Liem's air was flowing and the suit pressurizing. He took the tether from Liem's waist, and clipped it to his own belt. It would be awkward using the jetpack while carrying another man, but Matt turned and started back to the station.

But then the terrorist bomb exploded—bombs—a whole string of them. Along the rim of the station, in the hub, in the docking bay. All within two seconds of each other. The structures ripped open and fire shot out, only to be immediately quenched by the vacuum. Matthew saw a space-suited body flying out in his general direction. He aimed himself toward it and turned on the forward thrust, dragging Liem at his hip. Then the speaker at his ear started speaking with four different voices at once. Some of the people who were working outside had not gone back in and had not been injured by the explosions. They were all yelling over the common emergency frequency. Matt turned his transmitter from the private frequency, which only Barb and Liem could hear, to the emergency frequency so he could yell, too. He saw that the body he was flying toward was moving; he was not rescuing a corpse. "Hey, you!" he called. "You there, the one flying away from the station."

"We're all flying from the station, wise-guy," a voice said.

"No we're not," said another. "I'm still attached to my ship."

Then the one Matt was actually talking to turned his head toward him. But he did not say anything. Matt caught the astronaut with a thump and their velocities combined to aim them in a different direction.

"Are you all right?"

"Is that you, Rogers?" It was Ismail Iqbal. He could make out the face underneath the visor.

Then Liem started screaming in Matt's ear.

"Shut up!"

"No one said anything."

Matthew realized that only he could hear Liem and he changed his transmission frequency back again. "Shut up! We're okay. We're safe."

"I can't see! I can't see!" Liem kept screaming.

"Close your eyes, we'll get you back to a doctor. You'll be okay."

Someone else started talking. "No one answers inside. If there's anyone alive in there, they can't help us. They — they won't have much air." This voice started crying.

Once Ismail had fastened himself to Liem and Matthew, making a small triangular unit, they saw that they were moving away from the station rather quickly. Matt turned them so he was at the back, facing Unity, and Liem and Ismail had their backs turned to it. When he turned, he saw a corpse float by. She had no pressure suit on — had been flung from the station when it ripped open. Already, her body was swelling as the liquid vaporized under her skin. Freeze-dried coffee, he thought. Then he almost threw up.

"Rogers, look!" said Ismail, kicking the body aside.

Another astronaut was flailing their arms and legs frantically, head turned toward the island of three men. Matthew flew them in the right direction. Before they reached the astronaut, there was another explosion. The rocket fuel and liquid oxygen stored in separate tanks at the docking bay had been leaking out and mixing. The explosion ripped through the entire docking bay and through all the ships and human bodies nearby. Matthew and the others were now far enough away from Unity to be safe from the explosion.

In a moment, they reached the astronaut, but the arms kept flailing. There was only silence on the radio. Ismail flipped up the visor. The woman's lips were blue, her head jerking up and down. They searched over her suit and found a rip through the outer layers above her right hip. Underneath was an oxygen hose with a small puncture. She was getting some air but not much. Matthew covered the hole with his gloved hand. Ismail attached an auxiliary hose protruding from his suit to the same hose on hers. The hose was designed for just such a hook-up.

"Liem, do you have any putty cement or string or anything with the tools you still have?"

"I got some tape." Matt found the tape and covered the puncture.

Again he aimed for Unity and turned on the thrust. The space station was farther away than ever and it would be slow going with three passengers.

"Attach yourself to him… uh?"

"Denise," she gasped, still catching her breath. She hooked her tether to Ismail on one side and Liem on the other, forming a spaceship of sorts with their four bodies.

"What's been happening?" Liem asked.

"Turn your transmissions to emergency, Liem. The station was bombed. We didn't have more than a minute or two of warning."

"I looked straight into the sun. I can't see."

"We'll get some help soon enough."

"How?" snapped Denise. She turned her head to look at the station. The wheel was still rolling but now the entire station was also slowly toppling around a new axis. It was as if it were a bicycle wheel that had come loose on the way down a hill and now the wheel was spinning and tumbling and bouncing in slow-motion toward the bottom. The docking bay was now on the far side with the wheel facing them. It looked like the old symbol for Earth, with the cross-shape of the four spokes within the circle.

"Come on, Matthew, take us back to it. We can get some sort of help there."

"I am. The thrust is full." But he saw that the station looked smaller than it had a moment ago.

"We're going away from it!"

Matt turned off the thrust. "I'd better save the oxygen."

"What do you mean, 'save it'? Get us back there." Denise, like the others, was scared.

Matthew yelled. "The jetpack would run out of oxygen before we were half way there, and then we would run out of oxygen." He paused a moment then said, "We've got too much momentum going the wrong way. And besides, there's not much left there to get back to. We're probably the only ones alive."

"By yourself, with the jetpack you could make it," offered Ismail.

Matthew said nothing. He just bent to read everyone's oxygen gauge. Both Liem and Denise were running low. Matthew removed the jetpack from his back and began to examine it. The valve for filling the tanks was the right size to attach to the auxiliary hose on any of the pressure suits. Thank God for standard sizes and for mass production. He strapped the jetpack loosely to Liem's chest and connected the hose. When Liem's air was gone, he could be fed oxygen from the jetpack.

"Matthew," asked Ismail, "do you think you could use that jetpack to rotate us again? I want to be facing Earth."

"Why?"

"It's about time for my prayers."

Matt was shocked. "Does your stupid religion tell you that you have to do your daily prayers, even in a situation like this? Damn it, don't you know what's happening to us?"

"It is not a sin to miss one prayer. And of course it would be silly to pray when your life depended upon your doing something else. But there is nothing we can do now but wait."

They now knew that they were going to die.

Matt rotated the communion of four astronauts, attached with wire tethers, air hoses, and interlocked arms and legs, until Ismail was facing, if not exactly Mecca, at least Earth. Ismail shut off his transmitter and started his prayers. Several minutes passed in silence, then Liem began to scream. He's probably not even sure we're still here, thought Matt. Blind. No one talking. Nothing to even touch or feel. Matt took Liem's hand and squeezed it tight. He stopped screaming.

Matt looked back at the tiny space station. He could still see the cross of the spokes, and the cross reminded him of his guilt. Freeze-dried coffee—a terrible, evil thought to think about another human being. But although he remembered his sins, he felt no guilt now. Somehow, guilt seemed to have no place here. Regretfully, but resigned to it nevertheless, Matt realized something else: he still hated Ismail. And to hate is a sin, he thought. He wished he did not feel that way, but he did.

Matthew took the nourishment bar that was tucked in his helmet within reach of his lips, and a few sips of water from the tube that came up to his mouth—his final meal before he died.

The Gig of the Magi

One hundred and eighty-seven dollars. Not much for some people, but for Jack it meant months of grinding gigs, foregoing pub night with his friends, and abstaining from streaming movies. He did a budget, and estimated that it would take three months to save that much. Three months *if* no unexpected expenses arrived on his doorstep. But Jack had learned to expect unexpected expenses, because that's the way life was. You could not know *what* it might be—that was the *unexpected* part—but you could be sure that before long, some expenses would inevitably come calling.

One hundred and eighty-seven dollars. It had been six months since making the budget and he was still short of his goal.

In response to the situation, Jack did what he always did, what he needed to do: he sat down, opened one of the several freelancing platforms he was registered on, and searched for his next gig. But rather than watch him do that, let us look at his apartment. A bachelor suite that is hardly worthy describing. The bathroom had a toilet and shower—no bathtub. There was a kitchen and a living room, but with no clear boundary between them they were effectively a single, not very large room. There was a small wooden table just large enough to accommodate two plates if both wings were raised, and beside it, two mismatched kitchen chairs. The living room had a flat screen television, very old with dozens of dead pixels. There was a single futon that Jack slept on, but currently folded up into a comfy chair. Though he lived alone, Jack stripped his bed every morning and converted it into a chair, not wanting his living room to look like a bedroom throughout the day. And there was a large sofa, too big for his cramped apartment really. It had been a hassle getting it in the elevator and then a nightmare getting it through the apartment door. But it was long and deep and comfortable—the kind of sofa Jack imagined a family of four or five might have, and for that reason he liked it.

Jack struggled to get by. His situation had nothing to do with lack of effort: he worked hard. Or at least he worked hard when he was able to find work, but the economic system was what it was, and on top of that, bad luck had pulled the rug out from under him more than once.

However, you should not make the mistake of thinking that luck always runs bad. As Jack looked through job postings, he learned that the sewage treatment marshes in the county to the north were dying—bad luck for the people downstream, but good luck for Jack. The freelancing platform showed new gigs for environmental engineers, bioremediation troubleshooters, artificial aquatic ecosystem ecologists, and sewage crisis PR specialists. Jack studied bioremediation engineering in college, and since then he had worked a couple of short-term manual labor jobs at the old oxidation ponds in another town and gotten good reviews from the supervisor. So now, he prepared a bid and set his daily rate at twenty percent lower than he thought it should be. Then he lowered his rate a bit more and clicked Submit.

Twelve years earlier, college recruiters had presented Jack and his parents with statistics showing that ninety-two percent of their bioremediation engineering graduates had full-time work in the field within two years. What the recruiters did not know was that their statistics were out of date. Municipal authorities at sewage treatment facilities across the country had started downsizing, replacing permanent staff with contract workers and automated systems. By the time Jack graduated, the trickle of layoffs had become a flood and he found himself in a job market in which the supply of engineers more experienced than him far exceeded the meagre demand. But now, six years after graduating, he landed his first proper contract in his field: two weeks of work, and at a rate of pay higher than he ever got teaching high school science modules or counselling troubled youth!

It was the busiest two weeks he had had in a long time. He already had a recurring gig for the social engineering department of his own county's police department—two to three evenings a week mediating between youth street gangs—and he kept that. He was also on call as a plumber's assistant for emergency night duties, and got called in twice. By the end of the two weeks, he had helped bring the sewage marshes back to life, prevented a gang war, and brought the toilets in the men's restroom at Walmart back up to peak efficiency. He was exhausted, but his bank account was two-hundred and twenty dollars in the black.

He logged into Gradgrind, this time as a client rather than as a freelancer, and did a search. As the first screen of profiles appeared, he saw that the prices were scattered across a wide range, from ultradeluxe to suspiciously cheap. He sorted the listings by price, scrolled past a few of the most inexpensive, and then began sifting through the profiles, scrutinizing the bios, client reviews, photos, and statistics. There was an option to search without seeing profile pics—an option created for people who wanted not to be influenced by their own biases, but he guessed that no one ever used it. Then, as he scrolled, he saw the profile he remembered from six months earlier. It was her: the same photo, same description, and the same price—one hundred eighty-seven dollars for a five-hour session. One thing had changed. Six months ago she had two reviews; now she had three, with an average rating of 4.67 stars. She was obviously not as experienced as some of the others in the category, but she was in Jack's price range. More importantly, studying her profile he got a warm, hopeful, yearning kind of feeling.

"Why don't you just hire a proper sex worker?" his buddy Anton asked. "It's actually a better deal."

"I don't want a sex worker. I want a wife."

He tried to explain, but Anton refused to understand. Not that it mattered. Jack's heart was set on hiring a wife for the evening. So he placed the order, and once the freelancer confirmed his security background check, she accepted the job and they set a date. In the four days he had to prepare, Jack cleaned his apartment, bought two fifty-cent air fresheners, and double-checked the business hours of the ice cream place beside the park. During those four days he also had some gig work that helped keep his mind occupied: one night shift, two days, and three evenings—youth counselling, superstore plumbing emergency response, and as a test subject for medical research into nanotech antihistamines. Then on the day of the appointment, on his way home from a tiring afternoon at the allergy lab, his eyes itchy and his sinuses congested, he stopped to do something he seldom did: he bought fresh vegetables. And he still had enough money left over that they could stream a movie after dinner—he decided he would play that one by ear.

He got home with twenty minutes to spare, brushed his teeth, set out the food they would cook, checked the time, started to brush his teeth again, and then checked the time once more. Then he sat down and forced himself to try to meditate. A few minutes later, his intercom sounded. He buzzed her in, sat down for a few seconds, but then thought better of it and stood up again. He opened his apartment door and waited for her there in the doorway. Before long he began to wonder if she had gotten off on the wrong floor or if the elevator had gotten stuck. But then the bell chimed, the doors opened, and she stepped out into the corridor. When she got close enough for Jack to get a good look at her, he was not disappointed. It's not that she was stunningly beautiful, exceptionally sexy, or magnificently glamorous. She was none of those things, but she was pretty with bright eyes and a warm smile. They shook hands and he invited her in.

First, she explained, they needed to review the ground rules, and she drew his attention to the safety protocols that freelance wives used. "Not that I'm worried that you're a creep," she said apologetically. "But these precautions are there are for those rare occasions."

"It's okay—I totally understand. So 'Brenda'—your stage name or whatever you call it—that's part of the safety protocols?"

"That's right. For safety and privacy, Gradgrind insists that freelance spouses don't use their real name. But that's an opportunity for you. We can call me whatever you like."

"That's okay. Brenda is fine."

She raised her brows for a moment then smiled. "Gee, that's a first. But okay: Brenda it is. Now, I suggest that you try not to think of this as a date. We call it a 'marriage slice'."

She laid out the style options for the evening, and he chose "Honest marriage slice experience". The "Full immersion role play" style seemed too artificial to him— he wanted to be free to ask her about herself, her real self, and to be able to be himself. He wanted a marriage partner vibe while still being completely real, rather than playing pretend.

"So what would you like to do first?" she asked, as she swiped away the paperwork and put her tablet away.

"We could cook dinner together?"

"Perfect."

As they cooked, she got him talking about his work—his *works*—all the different kinds of freelancing he did. At one point he worried that he was boring her, but she seemed genuinely interested. As they ate, he was so stuffed up he could barely taste the food, but he hardly noticed, being absorbed in listening to "Brenda". He asked her what she did in her free time, and when she answered, he asked for more details. She was surprised that he was interested in her "boring hobbies", but it was easy for Jack to seem interested—because he actually was. The content of the conversation was typical first date fare, but to Jack, somehow the tone, the feeling of it all, was comfortably relaxed and familiar, the way he imagined it might be between two people married ten years and still very much in love.

As they started washing dishes, she described one of her pastimes. It was a project she participated in at her neighborhood community center: a team of volunteers who regularly engaged in internet pixie dusting. "It's the opposite of trolling," she explained. "Some of the others in the group specialize in finding issues and memes and to post about, and I mostly wordsmith the posts."

"So you're a writer?"

"Well, yeah. Sort of. I also… Never mind."

She seemed embarrassed. "What?" he asked. "What were you going to say?"

"Well, I also write stories," she muttered. "They're probably not very good. I don't know. It's just something I like to do."

He put down the plate he was drying and looked at her. "What kind of stories?"

"Mostly mysteries. Sometimes I try to be more, you know, 'literary', and write about emotional or ethical dilemmas, but mostly mysteries."

"That's great! So, like, short stories?"

"Mostly. But I even wrote a screenplay once, just for fun."

"Have you ever tried to do that professionally? The screenplays, I mean."

"Oh, no no. AIs have been doing all the screenwriting in Hollywood at least since the twenties."

"Oh, right. I didn't think of that. I guess that's 'cause I like old movies. There was more of a human touch back then maybe."

"So what about you? Do you have any hobbies?"

"No, not really. I don't get time. Or when I have time, I'm usually too tired." What he did not say was, "… or too broke."

"Your work then. Tell me more about that. What was your most interesting gig ever?"

"That's easy. I was Governor of Minnesota for ten days."

"You certainly have a wide-ranging set of skills."

"Not really. I got that one based on my experience with adolescents and my training in sewage treatment."

"That makes sense. But I bet your profile picture helped too. When I saw it, I thought, 'He looks like a young, successful politician.' But I don't think it suits you, actually. You're more handsome than your profile picture. More handsome and more real than a politician. That photo doesn't do you justice. Oh, don't blush—it's true. Anyway, tell me more. Governor: that's a big responsibility."

"Not as much as you might think. They don't let you decide anything important. That's why they switched it from being an elected position to part of the gig economy. Basically, I was mediating state representatives and—"

She sneezed. A cute, demure, dignified sneeze.

"Bless you. The state legislature was in deadlock and I—"

She sneezed again. "Excuse me."

On the third sneeze, Jack realized that he had not changed his clothes after returning home from an afternoon being subjected to allergy experiments. He decided that the best thing would be for both of them to get out in the open air, so he suggested they leave the rest of the dishes and go for a walk.

Her sneezing subsided by the time they reached the park, and the conversation continued. It felt free and natural. It felt good. He did not mind her runny nose, and luckily he had a whole packet of tissues that the lab had given him, but now he was worried that she would not have any fun. He suggested ice cream, but she said dairy would make her sinuses worse.

I've ruined everything, he thought. Why didn't I shower and change clothes when I got home?

But still she carried on, skillfully and professionally putting him at ease. Her smile continued to disarm him and she even responded to his dry humor, sometimes laughing, sometimes playing along with her own dry wit. He wished he had met her in real life rather than as client and freelancer. But he halted that train of thought. *She's just doing her job*, he told himself. *I don't even know her real name. Don't get carried away, Jack.*

When they got back to his apartment, she asked if he wanted them to finish the dishes or do some other housework together.

"Umm. Not really."

"Okay…" She looked down shyly. "Would you like to have sex?"

"Yeah, I suppose."

She raised an eyebrow.

"No! I mean I don't mean 'suppose'. I mean 'yes'. Definitely yes. What I mean is—"

She gently turned her palms upward and slowly raised them and then just as slowly let them drift down again—the international gesture for "take a deep breath".

He did. "What I mean is, yes, let's definitely do that. But we've got some time. Why don't we sit and watch a movie together first?"

She smiled at that, and this time the smile lingered. He picked a movie—an old romantic comedy from back in the days when the screenplays were written by humans. His sofa had deep seats, and about fifteen minutes into the movie, she told him to lean back into the shoulder of the sofa and then she turned her back and reclined into him. With a bit of shimmying they found a comfortable position and they stayed like that for the rest of the movie, her nose still running, him completely congested and forced to breathe through his mouth. Like that, exhausted from back-to-back shifts and thoroughly contented to have Brenda in his arms, he floated off to sleep.

When Jack awoke, the movie was over, long over, and Brenda (not her real name) was gone. He became angry with himself, angry that he had foolishly fallen asleep and wasted half the evening. He worried too that she might have interpreted his falling asleep as a sign of indifference or disrespect. He went to bed, replaying the evening in his mind, warmed by how good it was, but also scolding himself for having forgotten to gulp an energy drink when he got home from work, or to change his pollen-infused shirt. When he got up the next morning, the anger and the worry had faded, replaced by a strange, achy mix of feelings he could not make sense of. Before heading off to his gig for the day, he logged into Gradgrind and messaged an apology to her. Then he gave her a five-star review. He had to edit his written comments several times before they fit within the allotted space. Then the moment he hit Submit, a new notification popped up: she had already written a client review of him and now that his review of her was submitted, hers was released and public. She had given him a five-star client review accompanied by three words: "A real gentleman".

In the weeks that followed, the uncharacteristic flurry of work subsided back to its usual sporadic level. When he was not too busy *at* work or too tired *from* work, he thought about "Brenda". It felt wrong that he did not know her real name, and he was lonely, more lonely than ever. Yet somehow he did not regret that evening or the one hundred and eighty-seven dollars. He knew that he would meet someone, that he had a sea of love waiting to be let loose. So whenever Anton told him that the gang was going to the pub, he tried to go along if he had a few spare dollars, which was not often, and to meet people. For a while he also tried a dating site, and even met someone he found through the site for coffee, but he and the woman did not hit it off. Then money got tight again and he suspended his subscription.

One time, Anton set him up with a blind date. Not quite a date, because it was just meeting up at the pub with the gang, but both Jack and the woman had been prepped beforehand: "I think you'll like this person." Jack longed for it to be true. But the conversation was awkward and superficial and nothing like his evening with Brenda. Before long, both Jack and the woman had run out of that things to say.

Anton called him the next day and tried to be helpful. "Neuromatch," he said. "If that doesn't work for you, I don't know what will."

"I barely have enough money to even go out on a date — I don't want to waste it on another dating site."

"Neuromatch is different. You don't fill out some long questionnaire and then they calculate your compatibility. People aren't honest on those questionnaires. No, for Neuromatch you have go into their lab and they do gaze estimation with your eye movements and quantum entanglement MRI as they ask you questions and expose you to different sounds and images and stuff. This one is science, man! They use heavy duty science to find out who you really are, and who the other lonely hearts are, and then they can find you a *real* match."

Jack was skeptical, but he looked it up. He researched and read reviews. It all seemed to be above board and potentially more effective than other dating sites. He decided that he wanted to try. He checked the cost. It was more than two months of Fridays at the pub, more than a single evening with a freelance wife. *No matter*, he decided — he would just have to save up again. He set a goal that by Christmas he would salt away enough money to sign up for Neuromatch, and then he scoured the job sites and freelancing platforms. When he did get gigs, whether plumbing, or youth counselling, or sewage bioremediation, he remembered Brenda (not her real name) and how professional she was as a wife. In the same way, he tried to be a consummate professional, to give every assignment his utmost. But work was sporadic, and saving was impossible when he was barely able to pay his rent. When a nearby town hired him to stabilize the activated sludge ecosystem at its treatment ponds, he got the job done in half the time they expected and he showed them what had gone wrong so they could prevent the problem from returning. And then, because the work was done, they ended his contract early. Finally, he decided that he needed to add some additional lines of work to his repertoire, and tried to think of what he could do.

The answer came to him: freelance husband. The going rate for husbands was less than a third of what it was for wives, and he would have to price himself low until he had some experience, but he had to try something, and he thought maybe he could be good at it. When he created a new profile in Gradgrind, he decided not to use his "young politician" profile picture and instead found a photo from three years earlier when he had a beard. He did not look any younger in the photo, and he hoped the beard might make him look more "husbandy" to potential clients. Then he waited while Gradgrind ran background checks and screened him. Two days later when he was approved, he chose a pseudonym and began watching for postings from potential clients and applied to every one he saw, even the postings he guessed he had no chance of getting. In that time, gigs in his usual fields continued to come in from time to time, enough to let him pay his rent and buy food, but he saved next to nothing. By the middle of December he knew he was not going to be able to give himself the Christmas present of a Neuromatch membership.

And then, to his surprise, he landed his first husband gig. The client was a woman in her late twenties who wanted an evening of hanging out at home, cooking a meal together, going for a walk if it was not too cold, and maybe streaming a movie or playing some cards together. Her profile picture was hidden—apparently the option to hide profile pictures worked both ways and this woman wanted not to see or be seen until the day of their actual meeting. They agreed on December twenty-third. Jack prepared by watching educational shorts on active listening, on body language, and, just in case she was shy, on tricks for getting people to open up. Then, on the morning of the gig, he messaged the client one last question. "Do you want me to pick up some fresh vegetables or something for us to cook?"

She quickly replied. "Thanks but don't worry. I'll take care of that."

Nevertheless, that evening, on the way to the client's place, he did stop to buy a small tub of quality ice cream. If he had been wise, he would not have done that. It was not required: after all, he was the freelancer and she was the client—she should be the one to pay for niceties like ice cream. More importantly, he could not really afford it. But he thought it would be a nice touch, and whoever this client was, he wanted to give her an experience as memorable as what Brenda—not her real name—had given him.

The magi, as you know, were wise men who brought gifts to the Christ-child on the first Christmas. What is not widely known is that two of the three wise men were independent contractors—temp workers rather than regular magi. Most of the magi could not be bothered to make the long, arduous journey, so the task was delegated to poorly paid freelancers. But though their status in the eyes of the accredited, full-time magi was low, that was not an indicator of their actual wisdom or their worthiness to receive blessings. Because although they knew the gifts they brought were inadequate, those gifts were offered as a representation of what was in their hearts, and in return they received the blessing of meeting the Promised One in person.

Jack had not undertaken a long journey to go and pay homage to the newly born Christ, or brought a gift of gold or frankincense, but he did give of himself. He kept hope alive inside him, he persevered in his daily grind, and he had committed himself on this day to give this new client his best. By now, you may have guessed what happened. When the client opened her door, Jack's mind was surprised, but his heart was not—he was both surprised and not surprised to see that it was Brenda. Like the magi, Brenda (not her real name) had also persevered, given of herself, and nurtured hope. In these days, these two are the magi, for they were ready to truly give and, for that, in return they were blessed with the gift of each other, the gift of love. And of all gifts, this is the greatest.

This story is dedicated to O. Henry, my wife, and the various clients over the years who gave me five-star reviews.

Money, Wealth, and Soil

Lucas Romero and his team had become adept at making sense of anomalies that the SoilCoin algorithm sometimes spit out. This time, however, the incongruities were different from what they were used to and none of them could come up with an explanation that they believed might actually be right. What was clear was that the remote sensing data for this secluded, hundred-square-kilometer piece of land looked too good to be true. And if it looked too good to be true, it probably was. And *that* meant that once again someone was trying to game the SoilCoin system. For Lucas, there was no mystery in the motivations behind what was happening: people did what served their interest. The puzzle rather was how to point their greed in the right direction. With the Pre-CoP Science Meeting and the Panel of Arbitration only four weeks away, Lucas made a choice: he booked a flight to Canada, and made his way to northern Alberta and the territory of this remote First Nation, as some Canadian Indigenous groups called themselves. Now the First Nation's young manager, Daniel Erasmus, was taking

Lucas to see with his own two eyes what was causing the anomalies. As they drew closer to one of the hotspots Lucas had identified, he let the view from the passenger seat of the pickup truck—forest on the right side of the gravel road, pastureland on the left—calm his thoughts.

His phone vibrated, pulling him out of his reverie: a message from Mahalia de Guzman, the director of the UNCCD's SoilCoin program. He swore in Spanish under his breath, then opened the message. *"WTF are you doing in Canada!!!"* she wrote. *"Denier extremists killed two scientists from their envt ministry's soil finance program last year. Imagine what they'll do if they learn the UN is there."*

He typed a brief reply: *"I'm trying to save SoilCoin."*

Lucas set his phone on the stack of thin cardboard sheets that occupied the middle of the truck's bench seat and looked out again at the beauty of the landscape. He yearned to forget about the currency trading, global finance, and natural capital futures for a month and just go canoeing or hiking. Both his native Spain and his adopted home of Kenya had saved some beautiful slices of nature, but neither country had anything that could qualify as *wilderness* by these North American standards. Even here, though, the so-called "wilderness" had people, some working in it, some living in it, some exploiting it, some trying to take care of it. He also knew that the landscape here was changing. The prairie was moving northward: with the warming of the climate, boreal forest was giving way to mixed wood forest, mixed wood forest to parkland, and parkland to grassland. In most places, though, the old ecosystems were dying faster than the new ones could establish themselves, and where new grass-land was spreading into the southern limit of the forest, and new forest was spreading into the southern limit of the tundra, they were impoverished versions of their parent ecosystems. Agriculture too, having drawn down its soils to the point of bankruptcy, was also sliding northward.

His phone vibrated again—his boss had more to say. *"The Canadian AMBASSADOR and a lawyer from RFD and are demanding answers from the Executive Director. They think you're overstepping our mandate. You're in over your head!!!"*

RFD Eco-Investments, a Montreal-based natural capital speculator, had leased a large tract of land in this area from Daniel's community and the Alberta provincial government in an arrangement that Lucas did not really understand. What he did understand was that large expanses of land in rural and remote parts of Canada were now being converted from farming or forestry to "natural capital speculation" —investors leasing or buying land to earn money from carbon credits, watershed or habitat concessions payments and, increasingly, SoilCoin credits. As far as he was concerned, if arrangements like this led to soils actually being nursed back to health, they should be encouraged. But only if the renewal of soils was real. That was what he needed to confirm. For three weeks, however, ever since the anomaly detection routines had flagged this remote section of Alberta, people at RFD had been ignoring his emails and dodging his phone calls.

Daniel took one hand off the steering wheel and pointed ahead. "You're gonna lose reception when we get over the next hill. Want me to stop for a bit so you can finish your messages?"

Lucas took another look at the director's message. "No, let's keep going. I'll deal with this later." He slipped the phone back into his pocket.

As they crested the hill, Daniel gestured at the trees on his right. "This bit of forest here helped keep my family alive during the famine. I shot my first elk in there. I was twelve years old. Between the hunting, and the traditional harvesting, and our Nation's bison herd—together, those things helped us get through it. We still had six people die, but it would've been more people if not for us turning to our traditional foods."

That was a time Lucas avoided thinking about. He had been in his early twenties when the soil blight, and then food shortages, and then riots hit Spain. Since then, year after year, the soil blight continued to erupt around the world, and several countries seemed to be permanently on the cusp of famine.

"Dr. Romero, would you say that you guys—the UN, I mean—would you say that you've started to turn things around for erosion and for the soil blight?"

Lucas sighed. "Not yet." It seemed Daniel had been hoping for a different answer because for the next few minutes he was quiet.

Eventually, Lucas's eyes were drawn to the stack of letter-sized cardstock on the seat between them. He picked up one of the sheets and looked it. It was stamped with perforations that created six circular slugs that looked ready to be stamped out of the card. "What is this? There were stacks and stacks of these in the garage where the truck was parked."

"Blanks for drink cup lids."

"Drink cup… Like coffee cup lids?"

"Exactly. We inherited them from the Canwest paper mill about forty klicks from here. We won a court case against them for contaminating the watershed. But as we were winning the court case, this big chain of coffee shops went bankrupt, and they owed Canwest millions.

Canwest decided that their best option was to declare bankruptcy too."

"So instead of getting money from your court settlement, you got thousands of half-finished drink lids?"

"Not thousands. *Hundreds* of thousands. But not only drink lids—there were eight giant rolls of stock ready to be chopped into biodegradable, cellulose-based glitter."

"Glitter like for children's art projects?"

"Yeah, exactly." Lucas stared at him, not sure if the young man was pulling his leg. "It wasn't all bad," Daniel continued, as he steered to avoid a pothole. "We inherited the mill's machinery too. We blocked the road to the mill and prevented them from shipping it out until a court confirmed that now it belonged to us. Anyway, take these drink lids for instance." He tapped the stack of cards. "Because of these, I studied materials science at university. The writing was on the wall for plastic drink lids and plastic everything else, and there's so much you can do with cellulose fiber. Like these: before a press stamps these blanks into the shape of a lid, they can be overlain with a nanocrystal cellulose film, and instead of using pigments and dyes for color you can manipulate the nanostructure of the fibers."

"To create structural coloration."

"Exactly! You know about this stuff?"

"Not about manufacturing it. But some satellite remote sensing methods look for structural coloration. I know someone who used it to detect the New Zealand shield bug infestation last year."

"They could see insects from a satellite?"

"He wasn't seeing individual insects. But the infestation was so bad that the cumulative iridescence of the insects' wings showed up in the data."

"Very slick!"

For a few minutes more, Daniel peppered Lucas with questions—several of them quite insightful—about the SoilCoin system and the kinds of remote sensing data it relied on. Then he eased off the accelerator and turned onto what was little more than a trail. He drove more slowly now, another two hundred meters, then came to a stop. Lucas checked his GPS unit. Daniel had brought him to the middle of one of the areas with unbelievable readings.

Stepping down from the truck, Lucas immediately saw something out of place. At the beginning of the drive, in the spots where the land wasn't dominated by trees, there had been a diverse mix of grasses, forbs, and bushes, but here the ground was blanketed with a single type of plant. They were mostly between thirty and forty centimeters tall, a few of them just starting to flower.

"What's this?"

"That's the cover crop RFD planted. It's based on prairie coneflower."

"GMO?"

"Yeah."

Lucas crouched down and took out his phone to capture an image with his flora identification app, but then remembered that his phone had no network service. He captured the image anyway to upload it for analysis later. Then he reached into his backpack and pulled out a device that looked vaguely like a camera. He held it close to one of the leaves then tapped a button.

"The cover crop is supposed to improve soil moisture," Daniel explained, as Lucas read the display on the back of the sensor.

Lucas took a deep breath and slowly let it out, his suspicions confirmed. "What it actually improves is *the appearance* of improved soil moisture. It changes the reflectance of short wavelength infrared in a way that *appears to our algorithms* as improvements in soil moisture. And you see the way the leaves spread out? This isn't like clover or grass. With this, each individual plant hides a lot of bare soil without actually *reducing* bare soil, and it does it in a way that looks to the satellites as if soil moisture has gone up. We've been hearing about the idea, but this is the first time I've actually known it to be used."

"You're saying RFD engineered this plant specifically to hack the SoilCoin algorithm?"

"We'll have to run some tests," Lucas replied, his eyes still on the display of the infrared sensor. "But yes, that's my guess."

"Very slick! Very slick!"

Lucas looked up to see Daniel nodding and smiling. *He admires how RFD is gaming the system!* But then he admitted to himself that he admired it too—just a little. It was pure entrepreneurial ingenuity. The problem, however, was that planting this engineered crop across the landscape was not doing anything to actually address the soil crisis; it was just sucking credits out of the SoilCoin system and devaluing it a little more. Interventions like this would make the system just a little less trustworthy, would add a few more straws to the camel's back.

Then, in an instant, Daniel's expression flipped and he looked worried. "If your hunch is right, will RFD need to repay the SoilCoin credits it earned? They've been doing this for five years. Will they get fined or something?"

"That depends on the Canadian rules. SoilCoin doesn't pay RFD directly; it issues credits to national governments. But Canada might need to repay some credits, and certainly they'd want to pass that loss on to RFD. That's not really my area; my job is only about making sure the algorithms behind the SoilCoin system are scientifically solid."

"If you decide this is a loophole and you close it, RFD will probably lose interest in leasing land from us."

Lucas had not thought about this—he was fixated on the satellite data and the algorithm. "SoilCoin needs to incentivize *actual* improvements in soil health, not this."

"Sounds like the latest in a long line of what gets done to us. Canada comes along and says, 'You can't live there on the prairie anymore; you have to go live up north in the forest instead.' Then we get here and they say, 'Actually, we're giving most of the forest land to logging and paper companies.' Then the paper company pollutes the water and when they get caught, instead of compensating us, its owners say, 'Sorry. Bankrupt. Canwest doesn't exist anymore.'"

"That's really too—"

"Meanwhile, the climate crisis and the soil crisis are putting the ecosystems here through a meat grinder. And you guys say, 'We're gonna fix it by changing how money works.' So we try to play along, and we start earning money with carbon credits and SoilCoin, but now you're about to say, 'No. We're cutting off your SoilCoin.'"

Lucas heard the frustration in the Daniel's voice and began to imagine how he must be seeing it: *Here I am, a stranger from the UN parachuting into their community to gather evidence that will likely be used to close off a major flow of funds for them. A small, poor, and remote community. To them, RFD's lease is valuable, and I'm about to take it away.*

Seeing the anger in Daniel's eyes, Lucas also remembered his phone and the fact that he had no reception here. He had traveled with this stranger from the edge of nowhere off into the depths of nowhere, and now was telling him that he might be about to further impoverish him and his people. He considered lying, considered telling Daniel that he had nothing to worry about, but the truth was that this was a loophole in the SoilCoin system that he needed to close. But before Lucas had a chance to say anything, Daniel whirled around. Lucas followed his gaze and saw that someone was approaching on an ATV. With its electric engine, Lucas had not heard it at all; it had just appeared out of the forest like wolf.

Then, as it got closer, Daniel smiled. Its driver, a man who looked to be in his early fifties, stopped beside the truck and stepped off.

"Dr. Romero, this is Reggie Merrier, our chief."

Lucas offered a hand.

"Sorry I missed you this morning," the man said. "But I see Danny's taking care of you. As long as he doesn't get the two of you lost in the woods." He laughed, which started to put Lucas at ease. Then Daniel summarized for the chief what Lucas had told him about the RFD's cover crop and how it fooled the SoilCoin algorithm. The chief crouched down to take a closer look at one of the coneflower plants. "You know, Dr. Romero, your presence here has caused quite a stir. Since last night, RFD and the provincial Ministry of Energy, Natural Resources and Ecosystem Services have both contacted me at least three times. And this morning, even someone from the federal government. Normally, I can't get them to make time for even a thirty-minute Zoom, but now *they're* calling *me*. And Amelia Gagnon, RFD's ecosystem investments director—she's flying here from Montreal this evening."

"What do they all want?"

"Everyone's beating around the bush, but I think they're all trying to suggest that I should tell you you're not welcome."

"Oh." Lucas looked at the chief, then at Daniel, then down at his feet. Mahalia was right—he was in over his head. For a few seconds the only sound was the trill call of a red-winged blackbird.

Eventually, Daniel broke the silence. "We tried to be so careful in leasing part of our land to this company. We had an ecologist study what they were going to do. Our elders discussed it. The whole community debated it. The money is helping us, just like a temporary side-hustle, you know. It's just a lease—the land is still ours. In the short-term we're just trying to get by, but in the long-term, this land is our wealth. Dr. Romero, can you tell us, is RFD harming our land?"

"I can't tell you anything definitive on that—I'm just trying to ground-truth the satellite data. And even for that, it will take us a while to analyze it properly."

"But if you had to make an educated guess…"

Lucas now felt guilty for imagining, even for a moment, that Daniel might have been capable of doing something violent. *He's actually more concerned about protecting his community's land than he is about the money they're getting.* He told him the truth. "My guess is that it's not doing any harm. It's not particularly *helping* the soil or the ecosystem, but it's probably not doing any harm either."

Daniel visibly relaxed at hearing that, and Reggie nodded.

"I suppose you'll want to take some samples of the plant," Reggie said, "and some soil samples, too."

"That would be ideal. I want to measure how much moisture is actually in the leaves and in the soil. A couple of live specimens of the plant would be best."

"Sorry. I can't let you do that." Then before Lucas had a chance to say anything, Reggie added, "Our lease contract with RFD has all kinds of clauses about not harvesting or letting others harvest, about intellectual property and all that. So, I can't *let you*… take any samples." Reggie paused as if waiting to be sure that Lucas was properly listening. Then he shrugged dramatically. "But if Danny and I go over there to have a smoke and our backs are turned for a few minutes, we wouldn't necessarily know if somebody collected what they needed and put it in the back of the truck."

Suddenly Daniel had a huge grin. "Not to change the subject," he said, "but I got a shovel and some empty ice cream pails in the back of the truck in case anyone needed them. Just sayin'."

Lucas chuckled, having received the message. But his amusement did not last. He hated that yet another corporation was trying to game the SoilCoin algorithm. The soil crisis was real, and the SoilCoin system that was meant to create economic incentives to reverse the situation was itself being eroded little by little. Once Daniel and Reggie were was a suitable distance away, he collected a few small bottles of soil, and dug up two of the plants and put them into the ice cream pails, trying to think how he could get the analysis done in time for the Pre-CoP Science Meeting. The Soil Convention was in an arms race against companies like RFD Eco-Investments around the world. He was glad to have them as allies if they would actually work to restore soils—that was the entire aim of the convention and of SoilCoin credits—but for that to happen, the incentives had to be correct. Companies like RFD would not do it simply to save the planet. And for the business incentives to align with actual improvements in soil health, the algorithm had to be correct. If there was one thing that Lucas still had faith in, it was human greed; his job was to make sure that greed aligned with saving the planet instead of destroying it.

* * *

When he returned to Nairobi, it was clear from the understated, almost sad way in which Mahalia reprimanded him, that he had done serious damage to his long-term career prospects in the UN. "There are procedures for how we carry out activities within the member states," she chided him, "and you didn't follow them. You didn't even tell the Canadian government you were going there. So Lucas, here's the way this doesn't become a diplomatic incident: *our position* is that RFD and

Canada were simply playing by the rules as they were at the time, and in turn, *they'll* choose to overlook your actions."

Sometimes the politics and the inertia and the bureaucracy were too much to bear, and Lucas wondered, as he had multiple times before, if he would be better off in academia. He did not care about the drop in salary that leaving the UN would probably entail—what he wanted was to know that he was making a difference. But then, three weeks later, the conclusion of the Pre-CoP Science Meeting and the Panel of Arbitration gave him cause for hope. The panel accepted his team's evidence and ruled against all seventeen appeals that different national governments had filed arguing that the algorithm had shortchanged them. Then came the CoP itself, which passed a resolution requiring the algorithm to be updated annually instead of every five years, allowing loopholes that Lucas and his team uncovered to be closed more quickly. Within eighteen months of his trip to Canada, the official SoilCoin algorithm was differentiating genuine soil moisture improvements from the false signal created by plants engineered for unnatural spectral profiles.

Still, the fact that neither RFD Eco-Investments nor the Canadian government would be penalized irked him. He had read the latest global review and he knew the incentives needed to be stronger. The actions being motivated by SoilCoin and other policies and programs were restoring soils in many places, but not nearly as quickly as soils were dying elsewhere. To make matters worse, the more the international financial institutions pumped up the value of SoilCoin, the more incentive corporations and governments had to take shortcuts. Meanwhile, in the declining breadbaskets of Punjab, Saskatchewan, Western Australia, and Ukraine, erosion continued, and in the wetter climates like the Mississippi Valley and the paddies of Kerala, the soil blight fungus continued to spread.

His response was to work harder.

The next CoP was to be held in the United States, with the Pre-CoP Science Meeting hosted by the university in Madison, Wisconsin. Lucas planned to participate virtually, but Mahalia, recently promoted to executive director of the convention secretariat, organized an event to celebrate the successes of the Soil Convention. "You need to crawl out from under your bridge and go there in person," she said. "It all revolves around you and your team."

"It's too soon to celebrate," he told her. "We haven't solved anything yet."

She insisted, saying that although the event would be described as a celebration of the science, in reality it was a political event meant to deepen support for the convention and for SoilCoin specifically. "If we want more countries to really get behind this, we need to look like the winning team. And you need to be there smiling graciously and speaking diplomatically."

As much as he dreaded it, he knew that politics and ribbon-cutting and spin were all part of what was needed to make the SoilCoin system work. And so at the event, as he sat through the speeches from high level panelists, he tried not to squirm. The CEO of the World Wide Fund for Nature praised SoilCoin for helping to put an economic value on natural capital, and a Hollywood VR star—the goodwill ambassador—cooed that the global financial system was finally starting to account for environmental externalities and move in the direction of full-cost accounting.

"One tenth of one percent of full cost," Lucas muttered.

Then came the presentation that was hardest of all to listen to. He had not realized that Amelia Gagnon, the Ecosystem Investments Director of RFD was here—he had not reviewed the agenda for the event and had not seen her sitting up near the front of the room. Two years ago when he met her in northern Alberta, she had been calm and unapologetic about their use of plants specifically engineered to fool satellite observations. And clearly the tightening of the SoilCoin algorithm had not ended RFD's interest in ecosystem services markets.

Taking the podium, she praised the SoilCoin system, and then she complimented Lucas personally. "Two years ago when I first met Dr. Romero at one of our restoration sites in Canada, I was impressed by how important it was to him to ensure the SoilCoin system is objective, accurate, and rigorous. It seems appropriate that after this meeting I'm going to visit that same site again, where we're still investing in soil health—the same place where I first met him. But what's important here is that it's the rigor of the SoilCoin system that gives us confidence to keep investing in soil restoration. The SoilCoin Secretariat and the UNCCD as a whole, every year, you improve your remote sensing methods and improve the algorithm, and that keeps us on our toes. And that's the way it should be. But what's really important is that your work makes soil restoration a good investment for us."

As she returned to her seat to the sound of applause, she glanced at Lucas sitting at the back of the room.

Is she smirking? We caught them red-handed. Exposed them. If one of us should be smirking arrogantly, it should be me.

He did not enjoy it, but he did his duty and sat through all the formal presentations, and when called upon made some optimistic pronouncements. In the evening at a wine and cheese reception, he shook hands and mingled. The next morning, he was glad the fanfare had finished and that he could attend the actual scientific sessions. The first one started with an economist specializing in global datasets who outlined how every country that created its own environmental credits system based on SoilCoin assessments had seen an uptick in farmers losing land to international investors. Then an anthropologist described a community in Ethiopia whose traditional communal methods of ecosystem management began to earn SoilCoin credits for the government, some of which were passed down to the community institution. Lucas felt as if she was speaking directly and particularly to him as she described how the new influx of money led to growing mistrust by community members towards its leaders. She finished her presentation by explaining how, last month when she had returned to the community, she learned that it had split into three hostile factions and the traditional system had completely broken down.

Lucas recognized several people in the room, and he knew that many knew who he was: not quite the architect of the SoilCoin system, but certainly one of its chief engineers. In the Q&A that followed the presentations, discussion revolved around intrinsic versus extrinsic motivations, whether the financial incentives were crowding out spiritual, cultural and moral impulses, and what it would take to put sustainable use of land and ecosystems on a firm footing permanently. And then the chair of the session introduced Lucas and asked him for an insider's perspective.

"I've got faith in greed," Lucas said. "Love of nature, concern for generations not yet born—it's all wonderful, but it's money that will decide things in the end. We need SoilCoin to work."

"It better work," said the session chair. "The consequences of it not working are too frightening to think about."

That evening in his hotel room, Lucas reviewed the latest anomaly analysis: a spatial, spectral and temporal deep dive into the remote sensing data in a search for results that made no sense. One of the flagged sectors caught his eye: northwestern Alberta in Canada, north of the town of the Grand Prairie. He double-checked the location: it was the same place, the same Indigenous territory where RFD was leasing land! He cursed out loud in Spanish and then English and then Spanish again, but then he channeled his anger into determination. He had stopped them before; he would stop them again.

* * *

Lucas booked flights from Madison, connecting through Minneapolis and Calgary, for the morning after next. In the meantime, he studied the anomaly analysis. Whatever this was, it was different than before—clearly, they were not stupid enough to keep using the same GMO cover crop. And unlike two years ago, this time the effect was small and would yield only a tiny increase in SoilCoin credits. But something definitely was strange with the sudden appearance of point-source increases in microwave reflectivity and strange spectral lines in the visible spectrum scattered across the landscape.

They're probably still experimenting with some new trick. That means I can stop them before they even get out of the gate.

This time, he made no attempt to contact RFD or to arrange an appointment—he would just show up. He did send an email to Daniel Erasmus, though, thinking that once again he might need the First Nation's assistance. Two days later, with coordinates of the anomalies loaded into his GPS unit, he arrived at the area in a rental car. As he entered the First Nation's territory, he pulled over at one spot where the strange satellite readings were within a few meters of the road. Looking around, he saw nothing strange. This was a location where the forest had almost completely given way grassland. There were scattered aspen and poplar trees, various grasses and wildflowers, a few patties of bison dung, and sadly some roadside litter.

He double-checked the GPS location: he was in the right spot. He took readings with his infrared sensor, took photos of several plant species, and then picked up handfuls and soil and looked, felt, and sniffed. There was nothing that struck him as strange. He had hoped that the source of the anomalies would have made itself obvious, the way it had two years ago. Not finding any clues, he returned to his car and drove another half kilometer down the road to a spot where the anomalous readings were stronger and stretched for almost a kilometer beside the road. Again, there was nothing that looked out of place—just the same poplar trees, the same wildflowers, more bison patties, and more litter.

What a shame. So far from the cities and towns and from so-called "civilization", but the few people who are here can't be bothered to keep their rubbish in their car until they reach a bin.

He returned to the car again and continued driving. All along the road here, his data showed that he was driving beside an area where the anomalies were strongest, but still he saw nothing unusual. He checked that his phone had network, then called Daniel, but the call rang five times then went to voicemail. Having failed to find any smoking gun, Lucas decided he would nevertheless go and confront whomever he happened to find at the RFD office. When he arrived, he was thrilled to see that Amelia Gagnon was there—at the event, she had said she was coming here but had not said precisely when. But this was perfect—if he was going to confront one of them, he wanted it to be her. With her was RFD's site manager, whom he had also met two years earlier. The manager led him into the trailer home that was their field office and directed Lucas to a table, all the while peering at him.

"Why didn't you tell me in Madison you were coming here?" Amelia asked.

Lucas avoided answering immediately. He wanted to reel them in slowly, to watch their reactions as he gradually revealed that he knew they had started to cheat the system again. "I suppose you know," he explained as he sat, "that we're always updating our anomaly detection systems, looking for new ways people might try to fool the algorithm. Improvements in soil condition that are too good to be true. Unusually rapid transitions…. Fraud."

The site manager looked to Amelia for guidance but she seemed unconcerned. "Mmm-hmm."

Lucas looked at the site manager, but he was now taking his cue from Amelia, sitting quietly, his expression blank. Lucas tried again to bait them: "Although the main algorithm is open source, our anomaly detection systems are not. Machine learning, input from experts around the world—I'm amazed at how sensitive they've become."

Amelia remained quiet, waiting for Lucas to say more.

He lost patience. "Are you using any new GMOs?"

The site manager's poker face dissolved. "You know, you're really overstepping your mandate and—"

"It's all right," Amelia said. Then she looked Lucas in the eye. "Yes, we are. It's a variety of milk vetch—*Astragalus flexuosus*. It's leguminous but we've tweaked it to also put a bit more carbon into the soil, *as well* as nitrogen. We had the Ecosystem Services Branch of Environment and Climate Change Canada review it for us. They couldn't see any way that the SoilCoin protocols could deem it illegitimate. Anyway, it isn't much like the coneflower—that did have a unique spectral profile—but the modifications on this plant are all about increasing soil carbon. And most of the benefit will actually come after we're gone—the First Nation isn't renewing our lease. We've got less than two years left."

That surprised Lucas, but he decided it was irrelevant. Whatever tricks they were experimenting with here they would eventually take elsewhere.

"Even with the coneflower," the site manager added, "your own panel said we did nothing wrong."

Amelia nodded in agreement, then changed her tone. "Dr. Romero, why are you here?"

This was not going the way Lucas imagined it would. But he decided that even though he still did not know *how* they were doing it, it was time to reveal that he did know they were doing something. So without yet divulging the precise details of the anomaly detection, he told them this area had been flagged again. "The anomalies are all geolocated. Let's pick one of the coordinates I've found and go see what there is to see."

"Your mandate doesn't—"

Again Amelia interrupted the site manager, putting a hand on his shoulder. "Fine. We're doing nothing wrong. Can you bring up a map and show us where the flagged sites are?"

Lucas unrolled his tablet, opened the map and showed them the clusters of bright purple dots. As Amelia and the site manager studied it, Lucas studied the two of them. Then the site manager stood up and walked to the wall behind him, where a large paper map was pinned. He looked at the map on the wall, then back to Lucas's tablet, then back to the map.

"It's not our easement," he said.

"What?"

Amelia leaned back in her chair.

There's that maldita smirk again! Lucas thought.

The site manager waved his hand over the map. "This whole area belongs to the First Nation, but our lease-easement is only here." He ran his index finger across part of the top of the map and then down the left side halfway to the bottom. Then he pointed to one cluster of dots on Lucas's map, then returned to the wall and pointed to a *different* part of the paper map. "That cluster of yours is here. And that other cluster in your data is off my map somewhere over here." He pointed at a bit of blank wall a few centimeters to the right the map. "None of your '*anomalies*'"—he put an exaggerated emphasis on the word—"None of your *anomalies* are on land where we operate."

Lucas's contempt was swept away by panic as he tried to make sense of what he had just been told. The land RFD leased was only part of the First Nation's territory. And it was not the part where the new anomalies were located. His mind cast about for something to say, for an excuse he could give, an explanation he could provide for having showed up here unannounced making accusations—something he could say that would let him save face. Then the panic melted into embarrassment. He apologized.

Thankfully, neither Amelia nor the site manager insisted on an explanation or otherwise expressed the offense they certainly had a right to feel. At least not that Lucas could later remember. They both said a few things, but later as Lucas replayed the fiasco in his thoughts, he could not remember what else they had said.

"I'm sorry," he muttered one last time as he got in his car.

So what now? Go confront Danny Erasmus and his people? Go try to summon up some more indignation as I accuse them now? I don't even know how serious the problem is or have even a clue what the source of the strange readings might be. Mierda! I messed this up.

He tried to calm himself as he drove, and to decide on his next move. Trying again to act like a police detective interrogating a suspect was out of the question. What he was sure of was that he would need to calmly and carefully write an email to Amelia Gagnon to apologize properly. As for the unusual readings in the microwave and visible bands, he was a scientist, not a detective: he would go back to Nairobi, analyze them properly, and if necessary ask the Canadian officials to come here and do some field studies. He doubted if he should even go to the band office to meet Daniel as he had told him he would. He could just message him saying he had been called back to Nairobi. But that too did not feel right. Then he reached a T-junction and had to make a choice: left to the First Nation reserve or right and back to Grand Prairie and from there, home. He was not sure what he would do when he reached the community, but he turned left.

As he neared the main village, he remembered Reggie Merrier, the chief. Two years ago, they had stopped at his house. In Madrid or Nairobi, Lucas would never just show up at someone's home unannounced, but he had the impression that here, dropping in on someone was very normal. He found the chief sitting in front of his house at a picnic table.

"Dr. Romero! Danny told me you were coming. Have you seen him?"

"Not yet. My—umm—my meeting at RFD went faster than I thought it would so I'm early. Danny won't be expecting me yet."

The chief directed Lucas to sit, then closed his laptop and went inside and came back out with two coffee cups and a plate of muffins. Thankfully, he did not start questioning Lucas about his mission here, instead wanting to know about life in Kenya and the culture of rural communities there. They chatted about that for a while and then about Canadian politics and about melting glaciers. Eventually Lucas regained enough confidence to ask about the community's relationship with RFD. "I'm curious why you're not letting them renew their lease. Even though they're not doing their GMO coneflower anymore, I'm sure they're still making a profit."

"We need the land back. Our nation is growing, and our buffalo herd—*bison*, technically I guess—our bison herd is growing."

"Does your bison herd earn you as much as leasing the land to RFD?"

"No, no—on pure economics we should probably keep leasing that section to RFD."

"I guess there are tradeoffs, whatever you do."

"No, 'tradeoffs' is the wrong way to think about it. Tradeoffs disappear when you live right. We take care of our families, we take care of our community, and we take care of the land—all three, no tradeoffs. If some option is good for two of those but bad for the third, then it's just bad, plain and simple. No, for that land, for a while it made sense for our families, and for our community and for the land itself to lease it to RFD. But it's as if we sent it away to the city. Like a son who went away make some money in Toronto. But now it's time for that piece of land to come back to the family."

Lucas had to think for a while about that. The chief sipped his coffee.

"RFD needed it all fenced, right? To keep out your bison and even… elk… is that what they're called? They needed to keep all the big grazing species out."

"Yeah, they did. Getting bison onto that land now will be good for it."

"Yes, if you do it right," Lucas replied. "Using grazing animals to restore soils can work, but it's a long-term thing. And the types of improvements it brings aren't easily detected by SoilCoin. So even if you're you do it well, it probably won't earn you much SoilCoin credits."

"No offense, but for us SoilCoin isn't about taking care of the land. It's a…"

"A side-hustle?"

"Yeah! That's what Danny calls it."

"Aren't you going to miss the money you were getting from RFD?"

"We'll keep taking care of our land. If SoilCoin or the Canadian natural capital credits give us some money in the process, we'll gladly accept it, but that's not why we do it."

They talked for a while longer, and then Lucas said he should be leaving. "Please tell Danny I said hello, but I got what I needed at RFD this morning."

They said goodbye, and then Lucas got in his car and drove away. Twenty minutes later he came again to the kilometer-long stretch of road he had passed in the morning where the anomalies showed as particularly strong. And there on the other side of a barbed wire fence, for the first time in his life in person he saw bison, at least thirty of them. They had not been here earlier on his way into the area. He had to stop. When he stepped out of his car, for a long while he just stood there watching them in awe.

I thought they were just furry cows with humps, but the biggest ones look twice as big and three times as strong as any cow.

Then, on the ground, between him and the bison, just beyond the fence, he saw a glint of reflected sunlight, but then it was gone. He moved his head to the left and to the right and then saw it again. He could not tell what it was, but if he kept himself at the same relative angle between it and the sun he could see it. He crossed the road and the ditch and approached the barbed wire fence. As he did, he saw other glints of reflected light from various places. But it was hard to focus his attention on them with the bison now so close. Two of the animals were less than ten meters away and they began fidgeting.

I bet if they really wanted to, they could break through this fence like it was cobwebs.

He stood still. And then, while keeping the bison in his peripheral vision, he looked at what was causing the reflections. They were scattered around on the ground, circular disks slightly larger than his palm. A bit further down the line one was almost within arm's reach of the fence. He walked along the fence until he was as close as he could get and saw that it was still out of reach, but not by much. He looked at the bison and saw that they were bunching up—an instinctive reaction of mutual protection in response to his presence. The closest ones all seemed to be keeping an eye on him as they grazed. Very slowly, he bent down, pulled the middle strand of barbed wire up and pushed the bottom one down with one knee, then he poked his head through and then his shoulders. Then he crawled two more steps, reached out and grabbed the disk and then darted back through the fence. The nearest bison had turned to face him, but the rest just kept grazing peacefully.

Only when he had backed away from the fence, across the ditch to the road and his heartbeat slowed again, did Lucas look at what he had picked up. He remembered the places he had stopped on the way into the area in the morning, a few hundred meters further down the road. And he remembered the litter he had seen there—it was not aluminum cans or glass bottles or candy bar wrappers.

It was these same disks, weathered, discolored and partly decomposed at the other location, but that's what they were. Here in his hand he had a new one. It was light and seemed to be made of a thin, hard cardboard. And it was green, but not consistently. Instead it was iridescent, reflecting various shades of green, or from some angles bright white.

And he recollected as well his trip here two years earlier, and the rows and rows of boxes in the garage at the First Nation's office, and the stack of cardboard sheets in Daniel's truck. These disks were Daniel's blanks for drink cup lids. But unlike the blanks he had seen that day with Daniel, these ones now had nanocrystal films applied. Lucas did not need to do a spectrographic analysis—he already knew what he would see. Daniel would have selected the right structural coloration to apply based on what the SoilCoin algorithm wanted to see. The benefit in terms of credits would be small, and would probably not translate into more than a few thousand SoilCoin credits per year even if they scattered them over their whole territory.

But they already have the cardboard blanks and the machinery for the cellulose nanofilm, so this probably doesn't cost them anything. How many of these did he say they inherited from the bankrupt paper mill? Hundreds of thousands? Enough to last them a couple of years, I imagine.

Lucas recalled one of the presentations at the Pre-CoP Science Meeting in Madison. One of the complex sugar chains produced by the soil blight fungus polarized light in an unusual way. This gave him an idea for a remote sensing method for detecting it.

He examined the disk. "Slick!" he said. "Very slick!"

He threw it back toward the fence like a Frisbee, knowing it would biodegrade soon enough.

Chasing the Sun

Ever since Spirit Sun brought human beings from other worlds amongst the stars to this world, He has tested us. Like a hunter who separates the sick and weak animals from the herd, He uses His tests to separate those who are spiritually sick from those who are His true lovers. Two days ago, when I was a younger man and headman of the Cheshlom, Spirit Sun tested us. I had been named headman a fifth of a day before, and for my entire time as headman, life had been hard, with poor hunting on the land, fevers repeatedly making many of us sick, and, most recently, sporadic raids by bands of Night-chasers. As we crossed the Swahrting Plain, people began to talk of heading for Greenleaf Valley. In a council, about halfway across the plain, we discussed the alternatives.

"We are lagging in our chase of the sun," Qaartey Rett, the oldest man in the band, reminded us. Pointing to the horizon, he said, "Look! Less than half of the sun is visible. Have you not felt how cold it is? If we fall any further behind, we'll be swallowed by the night. Even though Greenleaf Valley is further south, travel is quicker there.

Both the collecting and the hunting are easier, so we can make good time."

"Moving further to the south will also take us further from the Night-chasers," my cousin Jaley added.

"What about the marshes and mud flats?" Braydon asked. "There is no way to be fast crossing the mud flats."

"You were less than half a day old when we passed through the valley last day," said Qaartey Rett. "To an impatient, half-day-old boy, crossing the mud flats seems like eternity, but in truth they slow us down for only four treks."

"I am more concerned about the Maltreylom than the mud flats," I said. "Ever since our two ancestors, Pish-Chesh and Pish-Maltrey, agreed to share Greenleaf Valley, we have alternated with the Maltreylom. Last day we followed the valley; this day they will be expecting to follow it. It's their turn and I think we should stay to the north of it on the Antelope Plain."

"It makes no sense to blindly follow agreements that Pish-Chesh made, when to do so means starving," argued Jaley. "Even if the Maltreylom have already passed through the valley, food is still likely to be more plentiful there than on the plain."

"You are our headman, now," Qaartey Rett told me, "but in this matter you are as inexperienced as young

Braydon there. You may be old enough to properly remember the last time through Greenleaf Valley, but you were not yet born two days ago when we crossed the Antelope Plain. Let me tell you, the collecting there is bad. Each day, the sun burns away the moisture, but when it begins to set and the air starts to cool, the rain falls elsewhere. It's dry rocks and scrub."

And so the discussion went, and in a short time the decision was made to pass not north of the highlands which lay ahead of us and thence onto the Antelope Plain, but to the south of the highlands toward the great, sun-following Greenleaf Valley. But even there, it turned out, the land was dry and food scarce. Then, about thirty treks into the valley, the Maltreylom saw us and attacked while we slept. Two people were killed before we had even rallied ourselves and found our weapons. We quickly learned, though, that the Maltreylom had been suffering even more severely than us. Many were sick, their numbers had declined, and they were no match for us, and so we drove them nightward and then southward up into the hills. Then we grouped ourselves together again and I resolved to take further revenge, for one of the two people they had killed was my brother Weslau. We made an unremitting push toward the sun, driving before us what little game there was in the valley. It was not an effective way to hunt, but it ensured that if the Maltreylom returned to the valley behind us there would be nothing in it for them. We did not see them again for some time.

But our victory and my revenge were both empty. The hunting and the collecting in the valley proved to be even worse than they had been on the Swahrting Plain. It seemed that the rains had almost completely missed this part of the world, and once again we were moving slowly because of the time it was taking to find food. Another twenty-five treks into the valley we came to the marshes and mud flats and found them dry. There was no need for the mud-shoes the women had made, and we walked across the barren flats in half a trek, instead of the four that it usually took. By the time we reached the end of the valley, three old people—Qaartey Rett and two women, Shaila Dan and Pawni Dan—were too sick and weak to carry on. We packed up our camp one trek and left them there sitting on the edge of the miserable river, singing the funeral song, left them to the night as we continued our chase of the sun.

* * *

When I was a boy, having made less than one journey around the world, I imagined that I would one day wrestle with the hawk spirit or the owl spirit, and take wings and the ability to fly back to our band. In truth, Qayruul-

Aatanaak could have given us the wings that would have liberated us from repeated wars with our neighbors, and saved us from an entire generation of enslavement to the Night-chasers, if only we had let him. Of course, it's always easier to know the best path when the sun is no longer in your eyes. To us, Qayruul-Aatanaak is known as Thapeylom Pisht, "The First Horseman" —although he was not really the first, he was the first we had ever seen— and his appearance had a disconcerting, soul-stirring effect on us. When we first saw him, though, he was still some distance away from our camp and we were not sure what we were seeing. Then, once he was closer, mothers began screaming for their children, and everyone fled, some hiding behind the shelters we had just finished setting up and some in the thicket of tall thumb grass nearby. This was a man being carried on the back of a horse!

To we Cheshlom, horses are one of the races of blessed people, so fast that for them keeping up with the setting sun as it circles the world is easy; so fast that they need have no fear of falling behind and being swallowed by the night, unlike human beings. So to see a man riding on the back of one these envied creatures was an awesome sight, and as he rode toward our camp, I watched from behind a large boulder, too terrified to come out, too enchanted to stay completely hidden, and somewhere within my racing thoughts I realized that atop that magnificent beast this man could chase the sun with ease. I realized that sitting on the back of that horse he would have the luxury of traveling one trek out of twenty and could use the other nineteen to hunt or to simply rest. Yet it was not our own amazement that gently melted our fear, but the way he carried himself. He rode toward us without haste or fear or anger, his eyes full of joy. Then, before he reached the edge of our camp, he stopped the horse and slid down from its back to walk, leading it by a rope that was tied loosely around its neck. Gradually, we began to come out from our hiding places.

"If Spirit Sun has led me well," he called out, "then I have found the Cheshlom. Please, come greet me, Cheshlom, for I have a joyous invitation for you!"

How strange, the news he brought to us: three of the bands to the north had united and all wars between them had ended. He told us, too, how Spirit Sun was remaking the races of human people and horse people, and how all this was happening under the guidance of the great teacher, Beautiful Sun. Although still a boy, I was old enough to understand what Qayruul-Aatanaak told us and old enough to remember the reactions of the elders. They listened intently to everything he had to say, but what they were most interested in was details of how horses had been captured and tamed. So Qayruul-Aatanaak told us stories of Beautiful Sun and how he had captured a horse in his youth, how he had tamed and trained it and then captured and tamed others until foals were born, and how these were more thoroughly trained. But in answering the elders' questions, Qayruul-Aatanaak, like a gentle grandfather, patiently directed the talk away from details of horsemanship and away from tales of Beautiful Sun's heroics, to tell us more of his teachings. Nevertheless, we marveled more in the revelation that the Wiisinalom, Volom, and Graalom each had over two dozen horses than in the fact that Beautiful Sun had united these three bands and was now their revered leader.

We had just set up camp in the shadow of Kalipantuu, the place of the three flat-top rocks, with only a sliver of the sun showing over the top of it. It was both unsettling and exhilarating to have the illusion that we had fallen behind in our chase of the sun and were surviving precariously on the edge of night. In fact, we were ahead of our usual position, and knew that as soon as we passed the crest of Kalipantuu the sun would be back in its place, with less than a quarter of its diameter hidden beneath the proper horizon. Because we were this far sunward it was a bit warmer than we were used to, and we were glad to have some shade for a few treks as we approached the mountain. It was there at the foot of Kalipantuu that Qayruul-Aatanaak introduced us to the teachings of Beautiful Sun, and then, after speaking to us and answering our questions for over half a trek, he tied his horse to a clump of tall thumb grass stalks and we all slept.

When I awoke, my father commented that I had slept a long time; yet, in looking up to the crest of Kalipantuu, it seemed to me that the sliver of remaining sun had not moved. Nevertheless, I went to sit with the others who were already awake, Qayruul-Aatanaak among them, to watch the last bit of the sun slowly sink behind the granite mountain. The younger children soon became restless waiting for this to happen, and their mothers took them away to collect yellowwing nuts and tender thumb grass shoots, but I was old enough to stay with the men to see this rare and humbling sight: the sun going down. It took a long time—almost a quarter of a trek—but when it finally set, Walit, our griot, sang the history of Kalipantuu. I knew that I would see this place again—two or three more times if I lived long enough—for I had been told that our people came here every day as we endlessly chased the sun around the world. The oldest one among us, Josha Rett, was five days old; he and the sun had been around the world five times since his birth, and he had seen the sun drop behind Kalipantuu five times. So it was not too much for me to hope to see the sight three or four times in my life.

Walit finished, and then Qayruul-Aatanaak spontaneously began singing his own song about the setting of the sun. His dialect was difficult to understand at times, but his voice was beautiful, like the howling of wolves. The song explained that in the spiritual land few people try to keep up to Spirit Sun, and so most are left in cold darkness, but that Spirit Sun's love for the human people is so strong that He always returns. At that time, most people still refuse to follow Spirit Sun and are again left in darkness, but those who do follow Him continue to be warmed by His love. When Qayruul-Aatanaak finished his song, we sat there, paralyzed by its beauty. Eventually the headman stood up, but even then we broke our camp in complete silence. With the song still echoing in my soul, I remembered the story I had often heard about Pish-Chesh, the first ancestor of the Cheshlom, and how he had promised that he would one day return, that those who followed him would be richly rewarded, that those who opposed him would be killed, and that those who ignored him would be relegated to the edge of night.

As we walked toward the crest of Kalipantuu, Qayruul-Aatanaak, that great apostle of Beautiful Sun, spoke more about Beautiful Sun's invitation. We were being asked to join the united bands. In a sixth of a day, about two thousand treks, we would come to the Great Sea, which we normally passed to the south of. Beautiful Sun was asking us to go to the north.

"That is the territory of the Graalom," the old man Josha Rett objected. "The way we maintain peace with our neighbors is to respect each other's territories."

I thought this a bit strange—even in my own lifetime, we had been to war with the Graalom twice and with our southern neighbor the Maltreylom six times, always over hunting rights and matters. But, as he walked, Qayruul-Aatanaak praised Josha's argument, saying, "It is good that you respect your neighbors' territories. Beautiful Sun teaches that this is very important. But he has declared that a great festival of the united bands will be held. Furthermore, the Graalom now ride horses and they will not be threatened by your presence." He nodded thoughtfully for a moment, then continued. "I think you do not yet truly understand what it means to live with horses. Before Beautiful Sun united our bands and taught us how to live with horses, we were prisoners, but did not know it. Now we are free. I have recently done what you could not possibly do—I turned and traveled away from the sun so that I could see the night. And once I had seen the night, I turned and rode toward the sun and followed your tracks until I caught up with you here."

"That's impossible!" Josha said.

At that, Qayruul-Aatanaak halted and reached into the antelope-skin bag that was draped over the back of his horse and he pulled out a bundle of wet furs, which he then unwrapped to reveal a glistening, white, crystalline ball. "You know that when the sun goes down, the air becomes cold and the water becomes ice. But I am sure that most of you have never seen this happen." He picked up the ball and held it front of Josha Rett. "This is ice."

People gasped and he broke off a small piece and held it in the palm of his other hand so that we could watch it slowly turn back into water. But before it had completely done so, he popped it into his mouth.

"Go ahead. Take a piece. This is cold water become ice." Then, as we all reached toward him to break off a piece, he added, "Do not worry about the Graalom wanting to attack you if you come to join the festival. If there is not enough food in the area, people will simply ride to the north, or to the south, or toward the sun, or even away from the sun, to bring back food."

I suddenly realized that with horses our band could have found a way around the marshes and mud flats in Greenleaf Valley. You see, we had emerged from the valley not long before, and my first experience with the mud flats had not been pleasant. Two treks in, I had gone exploring with my younger brother, Weslau. As we were walking, some distance from our camp, one of my mud-shoes slipped off and I fell. Instantly, my right leg was in up past the knee and my right arm almost to the shoulder. Stupidly, I struggled to get up, which only caused the mud to hold me tighter. My brother tried to pull me up but he was small and almost fell himself. Then he went to get help. Nothing in my life had been more terrifying than waiting there alone, but now, listening to Qayruul-Aatanaak, I began to hope that next time we could simply ride around the flats.

"And there is another reason for you to join us," he announced. "The Night-chasers."

This was the first we had heard of the "Night-chasers", and as Qayruul-Aatanaak told us of this powerful tribe of corrupt and cowardly souls, we were astonished: people from the other side of the world, where the day was just beginning, living their lives in reverse, people who every trek fled from the sun toward the night and its melting ice. It is an eerie thing to realize that wherever you are, half a day earlier when you were on the other side of the world, someone was already here, walking over the very spot where you are walking now. But now, Qayruul-Aatanaak told us, the Night-chasers had come over the top of the world and, with their greater numbers, had been waging war against the united bands' northern neighbors. "They will surely come to us next, and then, if we are defeated, to you. So if you wish to join us, then pass to the north of the Great Sea, and I promise that our horsemen will come to find you and direct you to the festival."

Our headman said that he and the other men would consult after we reached the top of Kalipantuu. But actually reaching the top was an event in itself, because as we got closer people began walking more briskly, until someone—my father as it happens—broke into a jog. Then other people started jogging and then running, and it became a race to see which of us would be the first to see the sun again. Although unable to keep up, I was still close enough to hear the shouts of celebration as my cousin Jaley ran into the light, followed closely by Shawnu and then several others. When I reached the spine of the ridge, completely out of breath, and saw our light of life, many of the older boys and young men who had been ahead of me were already gone, having begun to climb one of the three flat-top rocks that sat higher on the ridge a little to the south of us. A few others were just standing there, staring quietly at the sun. I sat on the ground and cried tears of joy.

Perhaps it was such joy that made our people arrogant, thinking that our traditional ways were sufficient, or perhaps it was the fact that we were ahead of our usual position in our chase of the sun, thinking that we did not need Qayruul-Aatanaak and Beautiful Sun and their tamed horses. Perhaps it was fear of the unknown. But for whatever reason, our elders rejected the invitation. Qayruul-Aatanaak looked as if he was ready to weep as he got onto the horse and left, riding ahead of us toward the sun, but we let him go, setting up our camp there at the top of Kalipantuu. Later, after we had all slept, it became obvious that Shawnu, a young man barely older than myself, had sneaked away to try to catch Qayruul-Aatanaak. We now know that our decision not to join Beautiful Sun had dark consequences for us in the spiritual land, but perhaps the fact that one person from our band heeded his call was just enough of a blessing to save us from total destruction.

* * *

About a third of a day later, by which time I had become a young man, we received a visit from two other of Beautiful Sun's disciples, and they told us of Beautiful Sun's teachings about unity, prayer, and love. Sadly, none of his teachings had any effect on us, and we again rejected Beautiful Sun's invitation to join the united bands. It was another half a day after that when, with me as headman, we took Greenleaf Valley from the Maltreylom, and were punished with hardship and starvation. Not long after leaving Qaartey Rett, Shaila Dan, and Pawni Dan to the night, we were found by four horsemen from the united bands.

"Cheshlom, it has been almost a full day since I left you," one of them announced, "and I fear that in that time you have become weak-minded in your heedlessness. You do not follow the sun, but rather the dim light of your own fancies."

Some people muttered surprised and angry replies, but Jaley, the first to realize who this was, shouted out, "Shawnu!"

"Yes. And I have come back to invite the Cheshlom once again to follow Spirit Sun's human spirit, Beautiful Sun."

"Why do you speak to us this way?" I asked him.

"You left us," someone else shouted. "You left us and joined another band, as if that horseman had taken you as his wife."

Shawnu ignored the insult and answered me. "We have heard of your war with the Maltreylom. If you had joined the united bands, you would have had horses by now and could have simply ridden away from starvation and from war with the Maltreylom and found places where the food was plentiful."

"Perhaps he *did* take you as his wife," Etomah called.

"Take your horses and go toward the night!" my wife, Kalia, shouted angrily.

I will admit that I was becoming angry as well. Shawnu had left us when he was barely more than one day old, and now he was here to scold us like children and to question our conflict with the Maltreylom when it was the Maltreylom who had attacked us while we slept and killed my brother. Without acknowledging the insults thrown at him, he further rebuked us. "Two other bands have joined the united bands, making us now five. But the Cheshlom are surely dead, frozen in the night. When the Night-chasers come for you, do not expect the united bands to come rescue the dead. But if you turn toward Spirit Sun, He will raise you from the—"

And suddenly, someone's javelin was in Shawnu's chest. The other horsemen tried to turn his horse around and to move away, but Jaley, Etomah, and then others charged them and pulled Shawnu down. The other three horsemen fled for their lives.

Three times in less than a day, we turned away from Spirit Sun. Qayruul-Aatanaak, who to us was the "First Horseman", invited us to join the united bands and Spirit

Sun's human spirit, Beautiful Sun, but we rejected the invitation. A third of a day later, we rejected the same invitation offered by two other disciples of Beautiful Sun, thinking that our own traditions and teachings were sufficient. Then we proved that we would not even respect our *own* teachings—we defiled Pish-Chesh's sacred covenant with Pish-Maltrey and took Greenleaf Valley from the Maltreylom. Spirit Sun, in His mercy, gave us a warning, forcing us to starve for many treks and to leave three people to the night before their time. And finally, with mercy that defies comprehension, Spirit Sun again provided us with an opportunity to follow His human spirit by sending us our own Shawnu. But instead of seeing Spirit Sun's compassion, we killed the only one of us who had turned toward Him.

Three hundred treks later, as we once again neared Kalipantuu, we were found by the Night-chasers—not a small band of Night-chasers as had raided us a few times before, but their entire assembled army. Their leader carried a ghoulish patchwork flag made from the clothing of the leader of every band they had ever conquered. They numbered in the thousands, with their strangely colored hair and frightening painted faces, and every one was on horseback. With such numbers, even had they been on foot, they would have had no difficulty subduing us. Spirit

Sun's punishment to us for having turned our back on Him three times in one day was enslavement to these lovers of the cold, these chasers of the night.

* * *

Survival under the Night-chasers was difficult, having to provide their horsemen with provisions whenever they appeared in our camp and at times having to care for their goats and receiving nothing for it except an occasional bit of milk. From time to time they would even take away some of our young boys, and raise them as Night-chasers to become their warriors. We were not allowed the luxury of showing compassion to our sick ones or to old people like I had now become. As I neared the age of four days, I began to find it almost impossible to keep up and knew that I was not contributing to the hunt in any meaningful way. My fingers, as you can see, are weak and gnarled, and I can't even make darts or javelin points while the others hunt, so when we neared the Swahrting Plain, where we would have to move quickly, crossing it before our supplies ran out, I sat down on a rock and began to sing the funeral song. The Cheshlom, a few of them weeping, left me enough food for a few treks and then continued chasing the sun.

It is a sad feeling being left alone and watching the sun slowly going down, and I became scared, remembering having been left alone in the mud as a boy. When you are left to the night you have a lot of time to think and to sing. I sang about our ancestor Pish-Chesh and his promise that he would one day return but that when he did only a few would recognize him. I know now that, in fact, he *did* return, and that we Cheshlom *did not* recognize him: Qayruul-Aatanaak, Shawnu, and others had invited us to follow Beautiful Sun and even to meet him in the days when he still walked amongst men, but three times we rejected the invitation.

Sitting there alone, I also thought about my stomach, and decided that I did not want to starve to death. "Let the cold night overtake me," I announced to the sun. "But let me not starve to have my skinny corpse eaten by wolves or vultures." And so, I started collecting in the area and, once I had picked it clean, I started walking. If I spent the whole trek walking and collecting I was able to get enough food—just barely—but of course I was not moving nearly fast enough to keep up with the sun.

For many treks I walked alone, and collected yellow-wing nuts, and even managed to trap a few small birds for meat. But, with the sun continuing to run from me, before long the air became very cold, any ponds of water that I found were covered with a skin of ice, and I walked with my furs wrapped around me at all times. Then one trek I saw ahead of me what I thought was a camp. As I drew nearer, though, I realized that it was not a camp, but the remnants of a battle, no more than a few treks earlier. There were seven dead horses and twelve dead men. I looked at each man's face and saw that none were Cheshlom, who by now must have been far sunward of here. Instead, the dead were all Night-chasers, except for one—a youth, dressed in the clothing of the Wiisinalom. There were hoof prints from countless horses, and protruding from the bodies of the dead Night-chasers were Wiisinalom arrows and Maltreylom darts, and immediately I knew that the united tribes had returned. The tracks and other signs suggested that a troop of their warriors had come, taken these Night-chasers by surprise, and, after defeating them, continued toward the north. Clearly they had been in a hurry: all kinds of food and weapons had been left behind, along with one Night-chaser horse, alive and uninjured, tied to another that was dead.

In two days of slavery I saw enough of the Night-chasers riding on horseback to have some idea of how it was done, and so, after collecting enough of the dead men's provisions to last me and the horse for many treks, I untied the creature, climbed on its back, and rode toward the thin slice of sun that was still visible above the horizon.

I won't claim that I was able to ride like a Night-chaser or like Qayruul-Aatanaak, but I still felt in my heart that I had gained the wings that I had longed for as a child, and I rode with determination to find the Cheshlom. By the time I reached Greenleaf Valley, four treks later, every bone in my body ached. Let me tell you, do not try to learn to ride a horse when you are old. But at least I was gaining on the sun, and the air was getting a little warmer. Once into the valley, I supplemented the provisions that I had taken by collecting nuts and by finding some grass for the horse, but still I rode every trek, taking little time for rest. Then, six treks into the valley (actually more than twenty treks' walking distance), I found the Cheshlom.

Our reunion was joyous, and since there were no Night-chasers accompanying them at the time, I told them everything about the dead horsemen and how I had found this horse. They told me about troops of horsemen they had seen from a distance, Night-chasers on one occasion and strangers on another, and those who were old enough to remember agreed with my assessment that the united bands had returned and that they and the Night-chasers were now at war. We continued walking, talking as we went. Some worried that a Night-chaser troop might arrive and find us with one of their horses. Others argued that it was time to break away from our enslavement.

Two treks later, after arriving at the edge of the mud flats, we rested, the women checking and rechecking the mud-shoes they had made. My horse seemed glad for the opportunity to recuperate, but it and we had only rested for one trek when a huge troop of Night-chaser horsemen appeared over the nightward horizon, riding hard toward us. The elders had not yet come to a final decision as to what we would do, but seeing the Night-chasers charging at us this way frightened us into a decision. We quickly put on our mud-shoes and, leaving my horse behind, headed into the flats, trying to hide ourselves in the tall reeds.

Then, at the sound of the screaming of Night-chaser horses and strange shouts from their men, I turned back to look: the first few to reach the mud flats had ridden straight in and now their horses were hopelessly trapped. Someone tried to stop me, but I went back, easily walking across the top of the mud with my mud-shoes, and I, an old man, got close enough to the leader of this troop of Night-chasers that he could have spat on me. He had tried to escape from his trapped horse and get back to the dry land, but now he was stuck, as well. There on the ground, just beyond his reach, was the flag he had been carrying. It was a hideous, motley thing made from the clothing of bands they had conquered, with sleeves protruding at strange angles and shoes sewn to collars, as if it were a costume made for a strange demon. And I knew that there was a Night-chaser somewhere who owned a flag with a piece of my cloak sewn to it, so I picked up this flag and stared proudly at the trapped warrior and then, without a word, turned and ran back into the reeds, taking the flag with me. The Night-chasers had no way to follow us and we left them there at the edge of the mud flats.

Four treks later, we had almost crossed the marshes and mud flats when a boy who had been walking ahead came running back to us. A battle was raging just beyond the marshes. Others were sent to see what was happening, and it became clear that the united bands had surrounded a large group Night-chasers and had them trapped against the sunward end of the marshes. Our deliberations did not take long—everyone knew what each other was thinking.

"Three times before, we had an opportunity to join the united bands of Beautiful Sun," I said. "Now we have a fourth opportunity. What will you do?"

"What do you think we should do?" the headman asked me.

"How can my advice help you? I'm old and have already been left to the night. You decide for yourselves."

That is what I said, but when they decided to join in the fight, I danced and laughed and sang. Then the young men collected their weapons and went to the attack. The Night-chasers were not ready for someone to emerge from the marshes behind them, and the united bands, with the help of the latest band to join them, the Cheshlom, defeated the Night-chasers' largest army.

As we have now learned, warfare and competing for territories is not allowed among the united bands. Each band is assigned a specific territory by the leadership council. Those who were among the first three have the best territories, but every band is given a territory on which it can survive. The Cheshlom are at the same latitude where we have always been, but nightward, behind the Maltreylom. After two full days, if our people have proven themselves and lived according the laws of Beautiful Sun, we will be given horses and the possibility of a better territory.

The stories say that when Beautiful Sun became old and was ready to die, his band did not leave him to the night. Instead, they gave him the fastest horse they had and he rode ahead of the band toward the sun. Some Cheshlom say that for having ignored Pish-Chesh when he returned in the form of Beautiful Sun, it is our punishment to be relegated here near the edge of night. I say it is not a punishment, but a mercy we do not merit. To be allowed to see even a quarter of the same sun that Beautiful Sun chased until his final breath is a bounty we do not deserve.

Afterword

If you have made it this far, perhaps you would like a little background on the stories in this collection.

"The Thursday Plan" was strongly influenced by my time in Africa. Not South Africa—I only visited that country for the first time some years after writing the story. But off and on, from 1986 through the '90s, and into the early 2000s, I was living in the Gambia and then Ghana. In those countries—in fact, across Africa—we had our eyes on South Africa and the inspiring work of Nelson Mandela and the anti-apartheid movement there. The demise of apartheid aroused a contagious hope, but still left us with an appreciation that to fashion a just world a lot of work remained.

"Problem Solving" is probably the most autobiographical of the stories in this collection. That may sound farfetched. After all, I'm not a Gambian; I'm a middle-class white dude from Canada. Nor have I ever been shanghaied. And as far as I know, I've never been abducted by aliens. But at the time I wrote the story, I was, like the main character D.K., a frustrated science fiction author wanting to write stories that reflected my dark view of the world.

"Communion" was my first science fiction publication. It was considerably influenced by "Kaleidoscope", a short story by the great Ray Bradbury.

There were a few currents that flowed into the writing of "The Gig of the Magi". I'll mention two. At the time I wrote it, I was between full-time jobs and trying to support my family through sporadic consulting contracts and gig work. I gained a bucketful of respect and sympathy for people who stay in the gig economy for the long haul. And in addition to that, in case it is not obvious, I'm a fan of the storytelling style of O. Henry.

As for "Money, Wealth, and Soil", the more that I've learned about the various environmental crises the world is facing, the more I've come to understand that we need to pay as much attention to soils as we do to climate change and biodiversity. This story is part of my attempt to take a hopeful but realistic look at the near future of these crises.

The first and last stories in this collection are obviously set on the same world, although they were written about fifteen years apart and are set many hundreds of years apart. Intrigued by the metaphor of the daily cycle of the sun as representing cycles in history and the spiritual rejuvenation of humanity, I filtered the metaphor through my interest in extrasolar astronomy, made the metaphor literal, and the result was "Chasing the Sun". But the question of how human beings first came to be on the planet Epsindi Ta and how those first colonists might have reacted to it had been nagging me, so eventually I wrote the prequel, "Five Days Until Sunset". Additional stories are suggesting themselves, so you may soon see more sequels, prequels, and sidequels. Writing those will be the best way I can think of to thank you for reading this far.

About the Author

As well as writing speculative fiction, Lance Robinson is an environmental social scientist whose research revolves around community-based approaches to land governance and natural resource management. He has lived and worked in several countries in the global south, more than a decade of that in Africa. Ideas from his research and his immersion in diverse cultures and landscapes often find their way into his fiction.

Currently he is back in Canada, living in Robinson-Superior Treaty territory on the traditional land of the Anishnaabeg peoples and Fort William First Nation in the city of Thunder Bay, Ontario.

His fiction first appeared in print in 1990. His story "Five Days Until Sunset" won first prize the quarterly *Writers of the Future* contest in 2023.

Follow Lance Robinson at

www.lancerobinsonwriter.com